# About the author

Larry G. Goldsmith is a financial forensic sleuth. He is a career licensed attorney, certified public accountant and financial forensic expert. Being a financial detective has led him to pursue writing fiction as a means to express his artistic side of his brain. Historical fiction is his passion as he revisits times and places long past while telling a romantic tale.

He brings a passion and skill to his storytelling, weaving his legal and sleuth knowledge. Like the author his characters are far from perfect, yet they remain ethical, good individuals seeking to pursue justice.

*Bashert* allowed the author to tell a forgotten tale when a few individuals changed the course of the world.

Larry is a member of various professional legal and accounting organizations and testifies in judicial proceedings as an expert witness in both federal and state courts. His hobbies include bicycling, writing, exploring other cultures and when younger, whitewater kayaking and volleyball.

# BASHERT

# Larry G. Goldsmith

## BASHERT

Vanguard Press

A CIP catalogue record for this title is
available from the British Library.

ISBN 978 1 80016 114 6

*Vanguard Press is an imprint of
Pegasus Elliot MacKenzie Publishers Ltd.*
www.pegasuspublishers.com

First Published in 2021

**Vanguard Press
Sheraton House Castle Park
Cambridge England**

Printed & Bound in Great Britain

# Dedication

My wife Mary Ellen, whose love and inspiration has supported me in every facet of my life.

# Acknowledgements

To my friends, Rabbi Vernon Kurtz, Eugene Goldfarb and Judd Stone, for their assistance. To Senator Henry Jackson, Congressman Charles A. Vanik, Natan Sharansky, the Soviet refuseniks, and the countless millions of people around the world who stood up to Soviet tyranny. Because of you, so many people today, live in freedom.

# Prologue

The days of my youth are only a memory. In the quiet of the night, I fondly think back on those days of innocence, as if they were yesterday. There were no cell phones or computers and yet, we survived. We had our music, our friends, and we had family. In those days, family and religious responsibilities were conscientiously observed. A man's word was his bond.

If his name was destroyed, his days on earth were numbered. He had the choice of two fates, neither of which was desirable. Jewish folklore tells us a 'good name' is all we really have, since it survives our death.

The Rav once told me about a man named Yankul who lived in a small Russian village. He was jealous of the respect the community lavished on its rabbi. So Yankul told disparaging, untrue rumors about the rabbi. Yankul's wife, hearing what her husband had done, demanded Yankul beg the rabbi for forgiveness.

Yankul went unwillingly to the rabbi's home to apologize. The rabbi was hurt that his name had been tarnished. He said, "Yankul, come with me to the roof of my house." They climbed the rickety ladder and once on the roof, the rabbi cut open a feather pillow. A gust of wind took the feathers and scattered them over miles of landscape.

The rabbi then said, "Yankul, I will forgive you, if you can gather and collect every single feather and replace them in the pillowcase."

Yankul shook his head in disbelief and said, "Rabbi, it's impossible. The feathers have traveled everywhere and anywhere."

"So, too, have the lies you told. They have traveled by mouth from one person to another and there is no way to repair the damage you have done to my reputation."

# Days of innocence

It was August 14, 1969, I am a criminal attorney named Michael Goldman and I was driving a borrowed, shiny blue 1968 Dodge Sportsman customized van with a white stripe running around the waist of the vehicle on my way to Bethel, New York.

Susan, my latest in a string of girlfriends, had promised to join me. She feared the damage to her reputation should anyone learn we cohabitated for three nights in a van and declined my invitation. She intimated that her answer would be different if we were engaged. I wasn't taking the bait.

Inside on the floor of the van there was a queen-size air mattress, next to it were a makeshift dining table and two ice chests that doubled as both seats and food storage containers. The van was cozy and perfect for a four day stay in the middle of nowhere.

I had stocked the van with food and drinks for Susan and me before she said she wasn't coming. There were times on the highway when I almost returned home, especially when I heard the weekend's weather forecast. It was personally unnerving going to a strange place alone. Yet, the twenty-eight-dollar ticket promised to be the best concert in modern times.

I needed this weekend to escape the all the bad news on the airwaves and my work created stress. I would not miss the evening news reports of the Vietnam War along with the depressing pictures of ravaging death and destruction or the stories of Jews being singly punished in the Soviet Union because they wanted religious freedom. Israel was in a war of attrition with Egypt; soldiers and pilots and the news of friends dying was overwhelmingly sad.

The world was in a chaotic state and society norms were discarded as my generation sought personal freedoms. Protests raged against the United States' involvement in the Southeast Asian War. The battleground of those supporting the war and those in opposition to government policies was being fought on the city streets and college campuses across America. The music on the radio allowed me to escape the work-related stress and grim headline news for the two-hour ride.

My AM/FM radio cut in and out due to the lousy reception in these hilly, rural areas, but it was my only companion. I would have preferred a female partner to pass the time, but maybe it is better this way.

The traffic was bumper to bumper as I neared Bethel. I parked on Hurd Road, about a half mile from Max Yasgur's Dairy Farm, known today as the Woodstock Concert Festival site. I arrived a day early, before the start of the concert to stake out a convenient parking place. I was close to the road and walking distance to the concert stage.

The sky was overcast, but the ground proved to be dry. I pulled out one of the two aluminum lawn chairs, placed it outside the parked van and spent the day working while sipping a refreshing beer. I made notes to legal briefs and reviewed court documents while munching on chips until it was too dark outside. Unlike the city, the country provided an uninhibited night sky bursting with bright stars for me to enjoy my outdoor dinner before I turned in sometime before midnight.

The next afternoon, I walked to reserve my place at the concert site. I positioned my chair facing the center of the soundstage about two hours before the first scheduled performer. I sat with a book, a six pack and snacks waiting for Richie Havens to take center stage. He played and delighted the crowds for hours. After Havens, lesser-known performers took the stage as the weather turned nasty.

Arlo Guthrie, a favorite of mine, was scheduled to play but due to heavy rains which began around midnight, I retreated toward the parked van. The agricultural fields quickly turned muddy as I slogged my way back with a chair and umbrella tucked under my arms.

Before I left the festival site, I noticed a girl in distress. Something drew me to her like a magnet. An inner voice in my soul told me that I must reach out to help her. People walked past her, as she sat sobbing in a puddle of mud. No one stopped to lend her a helping-hand. When I stooped down to offer her assistance, her angelic smile tugged at my heart.

# There was something special about her

She was a beautiful girl, sitting on the wet, muddy ground, sobbing. Her white sundress was now soiled. I felt an immediate sexual attraction. Call it providence or fate; it drew our souls to one another. I gazed into her dark, seductive eyes and I asked, "What's wrong?" I was suddenly struck by some force of nature. I forgot that I had a girlfriend named Susan. I was drawn to this enchanted soul and wanted to know everything about her.

A sad voice replied to me. "I lost my friend. I am cold, wet and hungry, can you help me?"

I reached out my hand to help her off the ground and handed her the umbrella. "It is a short walk to my van where I have dry clothes and food." Without a word she took my hand and walked with me.

On the way she began to talk gibberish; something about the colors of the falling rain drops. She then sang which seemed to cheer her up. Once inside the van I noticed her eyes were partially shut as her body swayed back and forth as if she was still listening to the music.

After I secured the door, I helped her unbutton her wet and muddy dress as rainwater dripped from her long dark hair and down her nose. Instinctively, I was drawn to her plush lips and kissed her. She in turn passionately kissed me. I threw off my wet clothes between kisses and tried to reach for towels.

With a glowing smile she looked at me and said, "My bashert, I have dreamed of this night all my life."

At the time, I didn't realize she had called me her soulmate or husband in Yiddish. I had a passionate sexually charged woman alone in my van who wanted sex. We dried ourselves off briefly as her dress dropped to the ground. I kicked the wet clothes off the air mattress. Her bra, my shirt and shorts were jettisoned to the side as my heart beat out of control. Eventually, I coaxed her onto the bed and nature took its course.

I must have climaxed three or four times that night. I found myself making love to a stranger, yet each stroke was slow and deliberate as if we were long-time lovers. I released my passion for her for the last time and she fell asleep in the comfort of my arms, her body cradled next to mine.

I stared at her naked silhouette and was mesmerized by her striking physical beauty. I had never had a lovemaking experience like that, despite having had numerous previous sexual partners. Somehow, as strange as it sounds, there was something magical about her and the way she made love cast a magnetic spell on me.

The next morning, I headed to the closest tree surrounded by bushes, thirty feet from the van to pee. I returned to the van, brushed my teeth with water drawn from the canteen and threw on an old gray T-shirt and plaid Bermuda shorts.

I allowed her to continue to sleep as she lay there with a sweet smile on her angelic face. I was mesmerized and hoped she would wake with an appetite for lovemaking. The rain outside continued to fall and I questioned if the concert would be cancelled.

When she awoke, she seemed disoriented, groggy and her speech was slurred. Initially, her eyes couldn't focus on her surroundings. Then, as she looked around, pieced together what we did last night and cried out. She looked down at her naked body and quickly pulled the sheets up tightly around her face, wailing into the fabric.

Her anguish appeared genuine, so I allowed to her cry for a few moments before interrupting her. "Your clothes are still soaked." I grabbed some of my clothes and handed them to her. "Here's a spare T-shirt and a pair of my gym shorts with a drawstring. I can make you some food once you wash up." With a smile I continued, "You can use my toothbrush."

She raised her head and her red, tear-soaked eyes. With trepidation in her voice she asked, "Who are you? Did we do it, last night?"

While she waited for my answer, she pulled the covers over her head, donned the T-shirt and pulled the shorts up, pulling the drawstrings as tight as they would go around her narrow waist.

She closed her eyes waiting for my reply. She was possibly praying. I responded by sheepishly nodding my head. "Yes, we did have sex."

Then, I introduced myself. "My name is Michael. We met last night." The lawyer in me prepared to proclaim a disclaimer: You willingly came back to my van with me. But instead, I said, "Yes, we made love." I paused to see her reaction before adding, "I have a twelve pack of cereal here, what would you like?"

She pointed to the Raisin Bran and then poked her head outside to wash her face with the canteen of water. She brushed her teeth, placing toothpaste on her index finger. While she was performing morning rituals, I cut open the box along the jagged edges, poured in some milk and placed a plastic spoon in the cereal container. We sat together at the table without saying a word, as each of us searched for words to express our thoughts.

Once we finished eating breakfast, she cleaned up, while I folded the mattress sheets. It was then that I noticed a bloody stain. Last evening, she had lost her innocence.

Noticing her wallet on the floor, I picked it up and learned her name was Shira. She lived in Brooklyn, was five feet and six inches tall and weighed one hundred and eighteen pounds. I didn't notice her birth date, or it just didn't register at the time. I picked up our clothes and put her wallet in the glove box for safekeeping.

We returned to the table. Reflecting on all that transpired, tears once again flowed down her face. She broke the silence with the following revelation. "I saved myself for marriage. I have never dated or kissed a man before last night. I dreamed I was in my husband's arms for the first time; it was our wedding night. My parents will disown me!"

Guilt overshadowed my vivid memories of last evening. As I handed her a napkin, to dry her tears, I couldn't stop focusing on her sad puppy-dog eyes. We sat quietly, looking at each other. I broke my silence by clearing my throat. "How did you get here? Did your parents know you were coming to this concert?"

"Devorah, my best friend at the girls' school, invited me to join her and her cousin for Shabbos. The cousin had a tent, and we were going to camp out and return to Brooklyn on Sunday. Devorah promised me everything would be properly chaperoned, and Shabbos would be appropriately observed. I told Emah, my mother, what Devorah had promised and asked her permission. Reluctantly, she approved." I remembered meaning of the word 'Emah' from Hebrew school.

Thoughts of statutory rape crossed my mind. Did I just have sex with an underaged high school student? I stuttered as I tried to speak, sweat poured from my forehead as I asked, "Are you in high school? How old are you?"

"My name is Shira. I graduated last June. I will be eighteen, the week before Rosh Hashanah."

I silently thanked God as I asked her to continue with her story. "How did you and your friend wind up here, in this place? What happened to your friend and her cousin?"

20

"Devorah's cousin drove us here on her way to Monticello, which I guess isn't far from here. Her cousin didn't stay, and my friend had invited others to share the tent with us including a yeshiva university student she had met over the summer. Devorah was involved in a serious secret relationship. She thoughtful enough to invite a boy for me."

Shira continued. "I wasn't planning to share a bed with anyone but my husband, and I was quite upset." She laughed sadly, as she glanced at the clothes she was wearing and realized she spent the night with a stranger after all. She took a sip of water and paused for a second. "I demanded Devorah correct the situation or arrange for someone to take me to a kosher place for Shabbos. I let her know I was furiously yelling as I didn't appreciate being deceived.

"Devorah tried to calm me down. She handed me a red or purple pill and said it would relax me. She ordered me to take it. Devorah promised that once I swallowed the pill, she would work on getting me private sleeping quarters. So, I took it. I remember seeing colors and then the dream I told you about before waking up naked here in your van. I don't know what happened to Devorah or my backpack with all my belongings."

"Shira, I think your friend probably gave you acid. It's also called LSD. Do you know what I am referring to?" Shira looked at me with a blank stare. I could tell she was clueless and clearly uninformed of such matters. She shook her head. Instead of trying to explain LSD, I decided to keep it simple. "Your friend gave you a potent and dangerous drug that causes people to hallucinate." I don't think she fully understood me, so I said, "The drug you took caused you to desire sex and lose your inhibitions. It clouded your judgment between what was right and wrong."

Shira thought about what I said. As she grasped the extent of her friend's treachery her fists became clenched, anger consumed her, and she shook her head. Tears of pain followed.

"You can stay here with me for the next couple of days if you have nowhere else to go. I will share my food and clothes with you. I will make no demands or expect sex in return. After the concert on Sunday, I will drive you home. There is something about you that intrigues me, and I truly wish you will stay so we could get to better know each other."

She sat there quietly for a couple of minutes and surprisingly said, "Thank you, I appreciate and accept your kind offer." She would later tell me that the sweetness of my soul reassured her of my sincerity regardless, she had had no other options but to stay with me.

It was past noon. I confessed that I brought a bottle of kosher wine to drink. For her sake, I asked her if she wanted me to recite the Shabbos kiddush prayer. She smiled. I placed a New York Yankee baseball cap on my head and recited the blessing. Then, the two of us shared Merlot wine from the same cup.

I blessed the challah, and we ate little pieces of the bread. I cut the remaining challah into slices and made peanut butter and jelly sandwiches for our lunch. I apologized for the lame meal but promised turkey cold cut sandwiches for dinner.

She laughed for the first time. "I haven't eaten a PB and J sandwich for Shabbos since I was five years old. As a kid, I hated whatever my Emah made for lunch, but my Aba said, 'Eat it or go hungry'. I went to my room hungry and fifteen minutes later, Emah would arrive with a sandwich and juice. My Emah even cut off the crusts for me. She made me promise not to tell my father, brothers and sisters."

After lunch, we walked over to the concert venue, dressed in ponchos, shorts and sandals. The rain persisted relentlessly the entire day as the music played. But somehow, neither of us seemed to mind. She had never heard modern music before that day. She found folk music to her liking. I thought to myself that she led such a sheltered life, yet in our conversations there was a thirst for knowledge to learn about what she hadn't experienced.

# Saturday's concert

Saturday's concert was scheduled to resume after dark. Due to the sheer numbers of concert goers, the promoter started it a little after noon. For as far as the eye could see, there were hundreds of thousands of people who had come here to revel at the concert of the century.

From the start, it was obvious the promoters were ill-equipped. There was a lack of food and water at the kiosks and about one porta-potty for every three thousand people. The toilet lines stretched for blocks. Most of the concertgoers wound up using the bushes and trees.

The attendees made the most of the rain. Some made a sport of sliding in the mud while others walked around half naked. The concert goers smoked pot, took drugs and engaged in sex in the open without caring that thousands of people watched them perform their personal acts in public. No one cared.

The rain radically influenced the concert. Microphones and speakers occasionally stopped working or malfunctioned in the rain. Later that night, someone from the Grateful Dead band received an electric shock when he touched the microphone, stunning the crowd.

Shira and I spent time talking about ourselves and then shared stories of our respective families. Slowly we were getting acquainted. As we talked, I could sense warmth in her words, so I took her hand in mine. At first, she was clearly uncomfortable touching me. Slowly, she relaxed and even smiled as our fingers became intertwined.

As midnight approached, we walked back to the van, through the fields of mud, broken glass and passed-out bodies strewn on the ground. The music continued to play in the background.

I tossed the ponchos and chairs into the front of the van to dry out and opened the windows to air it out. I made dinner while Shira set the table with paper plates, napkins, plastic knives and forks. I placed on the table mustard, pickles and potato chips to complement the cold turkey sandwiches. It was funny how she thought she was distracting me when she asked me to check if it was still raining outside. When she thought I wasn't watching, she sneaked a peek at the wrapper to make sure the turkey meat was indeed kosher.

She thanked me for the dinner meal and lightly kissed my cheek. I felt a personal connection developing and didn't want to blow it by rushing her. I surmised the kiss was the first one she had ever knowingly given to a guy.

We got ready for bed. I placed the sheets on the air mattress along with the pillows. I smelled the stench from my body, after a day in the scorching summer day

25

while wearing a plastic poncho. I knew I could not fall asleep unless I had a cleansing shower.

"Shira, I smell from wearing the poncho all day. I am going to take this bar of soap outside and shower in the pouring rain. If you want to wash yourself when I return, feel free. Otherwise, I recommend you use wet paper towels and soap before you lay on the clean sheets. Here's a fresh T-shirt to wear once you have cleaned up." I was direct with my comments.

With that, I undressed outside so not to embarrass her. I placed a towel near the back door of the van and showered as our ancestors did generations ago. The rainwater was cold, and goosebumps ran from my neck to my toes. I rubbed the soap on my body and scalp. Afterwards, I ran back to the van, and dried off. For her sake, I wore a T-shirt to bed.

When, I returned Shira was wrapped in a towel holding a handful of toilet paper in her hand. She opened her hand indicating she wanted the soap and asked, "Is anyone out there? Will anyone see me?" I shook my head no. Then she begged, "Please, promise me you won't look at me through the window."

"That's a hard promise to keep. You are so beautiful. But yes, I promise." I grinned and added, "Hurry, before I change my mind." I kept my promise.

As she re-entered the van, I handed her a clean T-shirt. Her wet, wild-looking, dark, curly hair turned me on. With the towel still wrapped around her body, she lowered the T-shirt before handing back the towel. I couldn't help but notice the erect nipples protruding from the shirt.

"God requires us to be modest. I wasn't comfortable showering outside in the open. I don't want anyone but my husband to see me like you have." I had remorse; I had changed her life forever, yet she had changed me, and I couldn't explain it at the time. I was under her spell.

We lay down on the air mattress. I initially placed my arm across her stomach and asked, "Shira, do you mind my arm holding you?" Hesitantly, she moved closer, and we cuddled.

Her body felt tense. I searched for a way to comfort her. I thought light conversation might do the trick. "Shira, let me guess. Your favorite three TV shows are: 'Bewitched', 'Courtship of Eddie's Father' and 'Green Acres'."

She looked at me and shook her head. "We don't have a television in our home. I have watched a show or two at friends, but I don't know the names of any of them."

"So, what do you do in your spare time and at night?"

"On Wednesday nights, I walk to the library and spend the evening reading. Other nights, I walk over to a girlfriend's house where we talk or work on homework together. On Thursday night, I help my mother bake challahs for Shabbos and help prepare meals for Friday night and Saturday." She took a deep breath. "Some evenings, I help my Emah prepare meals for a shiva family, you know, the seven days of mourning." I nodded my head. "Occasionally, I tutor children in English and in their Hebrew studies."

She was opening up to me and I wanted the dialog to continue. "On Shabbos what do you do?" As she talked, the tension in her body dissipated.

"I may stay at home and help my mother prepare meals and set the table for when the family returns, or I may go to shul and spend time with my girlfriends."

"I have never known anyone like you before. I'm impressed by your devotion to family and community. To change the subject, what books do you read? Don't tell me you only read Jewish history books?"

She laughed. "No, I love reading romance novels, travel books and the 'National Geographic' magazine to learn about exotic places." As she shared her life with me, I started to realize how different she was from anyone I had known and how special she was. My attraction for her grew.

"Shira, I had the most marvelous day with you today." Her fingers played with my hair. Her lips grew closer to mine and her lips kissed my lips. At that moment, my heart began to race, and my penis reacted too, but I controlled my desires.

"Michael, I wish I could run away with you rather than face my parents in the coming days. I betrayed their trust. Two days ago, I would have never thought I would share a bed with someone other than my husband. Now, well, look at us. Would you mind just holding me tonight?" She must have sensed my sexual desires.

We fell asleep holding each other. I can't tell you how much my body craved her touch. I wanted to feel her and smell her as she became sexually aroused. To this day, I do not know how I was able to restrain myself. I would like to think I respected her too much to violate her again. If she had allowed me, I would have made love with her all night long.

# Sunday

I woke up early and was the first to see the light of day. I went over to the rearview mirror where Shira's bra was hanging. I had hand-washed the mud from her underwear with the bar of soap while she was sleeping the night before.

Her eyes opened, her face so peaceful, I hated to wake her. "Michael, good morning, how did you sleep?" I handed her the undergarments.

"I slept well." Then I had to say, "My mother wears underwear like yours. For your birthday, I'll have to buy you something a little sexier."

She grabbed the undergarments out of my hand and dove under the sheets with them. As she dressed, she asked with reservation, "It feels strange. I guess we are returning to the real world today. I wonder what will happen to us?"

As we munched on Sugar Frosted Flakes (we had run out of Raisin Bran), I confessed. "I want to see more of you when we return home. I want your phone number and spend as much time together as we can."

She smirked and said, "You just don't understand. My three sisters and two brothers had arranged marriages. The matchmaker sat down with my parents and siblings and discussed qualities they wanted from an intended spousal candidate." She sighed. "The matchmaker made a list of the best candidates and asked the prospective match's family if they would be open to pursue marriage discussions.

"A match would then be invited to my parents' home. The couple would talk for an hour. Depending on their mutual feelings of compatibility they would pursue a relationship. After two or three chaperoned dates, a wedding would be scheduled, or the couple pursued other marital prospects. Being religious, we are only permitted to hold hands or kiss after the wedding. Physical expressions of endearment are only reserved for our spouse, children and parents."

Shira continued to explain. "Each of my siblings were married by their nineteen birthday and were parents the following year." The tone of her voice turned sad as she said, "I had hoped to attend Stern College to pursue education and literary degrees this fall. Who knows what will become of me now? Only my two brothers attended college. I was shocked when my Aba gave me permission to attend the university."

"My brother Yehuda graduated with an accounting degree, and Yeshmel with a business management degree."

As I listened to her, there were questions that ate away in my gut. Finally, I blurted out, "Do you have romantic feelings for me? It has only been two days, but do you want to see me after today? Do we have a future?

If yes, let me go to your parents and ask them for permission for us to date."

There was dead silence. The only sound I heard was raindrops hitting the roof of the van. I was getting worried that our relationship might end once we left Woodstock. She must have been thinking how she could explain me to her parents. It would be so much easier for her if she never saw me again. I noticed she was biting her lower lip as she contemplated her next sentence.

"Michael, the last two days with you have changed my life." I thought to myself that the familiar 'I just want to be a friend speech' was about to be delivered. "My feelings for you are real, but you can't call my home. If you give me your telephone number, I will call you every night that I can after my mother goes to bed."

"Shira, I will take it slow, but I want to see you at least once a week." I said slow, but I didn't really mean it. I already physically desired her again and just thinking about her caused my passions to be reignited. I was like a giddy schoolboy suffering the heat of his first puppy-love as I looked into her eyes.

"Michael, if my parents throw me out of the house, I may need to live with you." She wasn't being overly dramatic. Crying and shaking her head, she added, "You don't know how afraid I am. I fear being disowned by my parents. People in my community will look at me with contempt and the rumors would fly like the birds if they knew what we did. Losing my virginity, means I

32

dishonored my family and would be an unsuitable bride-to-be. My life is ruined, and it will never be the same."

"Shira let's go back to the city. On the way, let's try to come up with a solution acceptable to both of us."

She smirked, "I can't go home wearing your shorts and T-shirt and I can't walk in the front door wearing a mud-stained dress."

"Don't worry, trust me." Then, I changed the subject in hopes of brightening her mood. "Tell me about your mom. What kind of person is she?"

"My Emah is an exceptional woman. Being the wife of a rabbi, she is expected to organize women's events and bring food to the sick and elderly. She is a therapist for women who have personal issues, and a terrific Mom raising five children. I hope to someday obtain my mother's praiseworthy qualities."

Having exhausted the topic of her mother, I asked her to describe her father. "My Aba is a Kabbalistic rabbi. He oversees the Bol Shuva Yeshiva in Flatbush and is the chief rabbi at our shul in Brooklyn on Avenue L. He is a rabbi's rabbi known affectionately as 'Rav' by his friends and acquaintances.

"Jews and non-Jews from all over the world make appointments to meet and consult with him. They say he has tremendous spiritual insight." She lowered her voice and continued, "My actions this weekend, are an embarrassment to my family. I betrayed Aba's and Emah's trust. There is nothing I can do now to turn back the clock."

The lawyer in me questioned if Shira's admiration for her parents was slightly exaggerated. Regardless, I didn't know how hers, or any father would react if he found out his youngest daughter lost her virginity by a man ten years her senior. Would he demand a shotgun wedding or simply shoot me?

As soon as she mentioned Flatbush, I pictured a stereotypical orthodox rabbi who spoke in a Yiddish accent, sporting a lengthy, scraggly gray beard, attired in a long, black coat and hat. Many of the shuls in Williamsburg and Flatbush were formed by immigrants from towns or areas in Russia or Eastern Europe. The pictures conjured in mind were from stories my Mom told me about her childhood in Brooklyn which she ran away from.

For the next hour, we traveled on the congested road from the festival site towards home, Shira delighted in telling me stories about her family and mother. She described her mother as a woman who served the community and even helped find safe places for battered women and children. I noticed her smile returned and the wrinkles on her face disappeared as she took pride telling me about her family. I was humbled as I listened, then, I questioned if I was worthy of her. Was I the person that God would choose for her? I was afraid that I wasn't.

"Michael, it seems I'm always doing the talking. Why is that?"

"I guess, as an attorney, I've been taught to ask the

questions. I've always been guarded: I feared letting others get too close and hurt me." I laughed and continued. "I can't believe I told you something so personal, so soon."

"So, tell me about your mom and your father. Are you close to them?"

"My mom's name is Barbara. Like yours, she is a stay-at-home mom. She volunteers and is active with Pioneer Women, a Zionist women's organization. Mom is always on the go and she has more energy than me. She seldom cooks; it's just her and she can't stand being alone in the house since Dad passed.

"Mom's dad was orthodox and lived with us until his death some eighteen years ago. I was ten years old at the time. After he died, the house wasn't as kosher as it was while he was alive. After his passing, Mom suffered from depression for several years which only speaks to the love she had for him.

"I guess it was during that time when my parents drifted apart and their love for each other withered. Losing her love sealed his fate and last year he died. He was disappointed when they were unable to rekindle the romance they once had. After his death, Mom was lost, but found comfort spending time with her girlfriends, my sister Carol and her kids."

The time in the van passed quickly and before I knew it, we arrived in Brooklyn. I had mixed emotions. If I could, I would run off with her and make a new life. I parked in front of Lou's Cleaners. It was Sunday and surprisingly there was an available parking space. As I got out of the vehicle, I noticed all the cigarette butts and soda bottles littering the curb.

I grabbed her soiled dress from the back seat and upon entering the cleaners, I was smacked in the face with extremely hot, dry air. Numerous fans, including a three-foot tall commercial fan oscillating in front of the opened back door were unable to make the indoor conditions bearable. The cashier wiped the sweat from the back of her neck as I asked, "Can I have this dress cleaned and pressed in the next two hours?"

In a distinctive Brooklyn uneducated accent, the employee replied while chewing gum, "We can have it for you tomorrow after 2 p.m. and it will cost $2.95."

"Is the owner available? I want to ask him a question."

A short, older man, with glasses hung around his neck, approached me with a spool of thread in his right hand. He had a soft European accent. "I'm the owner. May I be of service?"

"I'm in a dilemma. My girlfriend can't go home wearing this soiled dress. Is it possible for it to be cleaned and pressed in two hours? I would appreciate it and would be willing to pay extra for your service."

He took the dress from my hand. He felt the material, looked at the dirt stains through his reading glasses. I presumed his name was Lou as he tried to hide his smile. He appeared to have assumed the obvious that I couldn't take my girlfriend home in this dress looking as it did. "I can have it for you in two hours, but it will cost ten dollars."

I felt relieved and burst out saying, "Thank you! You're a lifesaver. I will see you in two hours."

I returned to the van. "Shira, they will have your dress cleaned and ready to wear in two hours. In the meanwhile, you need to come with me. I want to take you somewhere." She gave me the evil eye, weary of where I wanted her to go. I said, "Trust me."

"Michael, I am not properly attired, if anyone should see me."

I laughed and said, "Don't worry about the way you look. Not even your mother will recognize you dressed in my clothes." She looked at herself in the car's mirror and began to laugh.

We walked into Magnificent Hair Stylists. It was a newly opened salon on Nostrand Avenue. The air conditioning unit operating above the front door was leaking water. I walked in and almost choked from the toxic chemical fumes. Immediately, in the corner of my eye, I noticed my mom's former hair stylist. She was older than I remembered. I walked past the receptionist and up to Connie and introduced myself. She smiled when I mentioned Mom. I asked her if she had time to help Shira. She said, "Sure."

Shira sat in Connie's chair. Connie told the receptionist that the walk-in was her client. The receptionist wrote something down in the desk calendar.

As I waited for Connie to return, I observed there

were two chairs to the left of her station and three to the right of Shira. All the stylists wore fancy, flaming pink uniforms. Each worked at a chair made of pink vinyl. The pink seemed to clash with the red linoleum tile floor and the navy-blue wallpaper. Shira sat facing Connie's mirror. On the other side of the room stood individual hair-drying machines.

Shira whispered in my ear. "Michael, I don't have any money to pay for this. How can I repay you?"

"Shira, you can't go home looking like this. Don't worry, seeing you will be my reward."

She nodded, stood up and put her arms around me and thanked me with an endearing hug. Then, she raised her head, closed her eyes and planted a satisfying kiss on my lips. I watched as she sat back down in the chair, now facing me, which then moved forward to allow her head to be lowered into the hair-washing basin.

Connie washed and trimmed Shira's hair and shaped her eyebrows. Afterwards, Shira received a manicure. I looked at my watch and noticed two hours had passed. I quickly sneaked out of the salon to retrieve her dress from the cleaners.

When I returned for her, Shira looked more beautiful than before. I thanked Connie and slipped her an extra tip. I had Shira's clean dress in hand as we walked back to the van where she hopped in the back and changed. She emerged from the van a new person, transformed into a young religious woman once again. I thought to myself, what am I getting into, falling for such a young religious girl? And a girl ten years younger; how crazy was this?

As I gazed at her, these thoughts hit me: her beauty transcends her body; it emanates from her soul. She is the most attractive person I had ever known. Or was I simply wallowing in guilt? How could I date a girl who was in high school last year? What kind of conversations can we have? If it's lust, will I tire of her? Are our lives so different that a lasting relationship is impossible?

"Michael, at the salon I had time to think. I want to be with you and pursue a relationship. I loathe deceiving my parents but will because of my feelings for you. On Wednesday afternoons, I normally go to the library and read until it closes at 9 p.m. What if I were to meet you at your office, say at 4 p.m.? We could go for an early dinner?"

I nodded my head with delight. Since she was willing to take the risk to see me, I would find out if this was a dream or reality. We jumped back in the vehicle for the final leg of the beginning of our journey.

Shira lived with her parents near Ocean Parkway on M Street, not far from Coney Island in Midwood, Brooklyn. As I approached her neighborhood, I noticed trash piled up. Mondays must have been garbage day in Midwood. I drove within three blocks of her home, stopped the van to let her out. Before she could escape, I told her, "I can't wait until Wednesday! Please call me tomorrow night!"

She blew me a kiss. Tears welled in her eyes as she left the van. "Michael, I'm going to miss you. I was hoping we would never part." I stood by the van and watched as she walked slowly out of sight. I prayed she would call, and we would have a future as crazy as that sounded.

# Dating a religious girl

I slept in on Monday and worked from home in my shorts and T-shirt. In the afternoon, I called the office for messages. I returned client phone calls and booked appointments before I turned in early.

On Tuesday, I was back to work. Susan called me at the office. "Hi... yes, the concert was great... Well, I haven't been avoiding you... I would have called you earlier but... No, I'm not angry. I haven't called you because I started dating a young woman that I met at the concert... No, Susan, it was not like that. I fell for her and it wasn't something I planned. If not for you, I would have never met her. She's young... She's ten years younger. I'm sorry... Yes, I understand." Is Susan right, I thought? What do I really have in common with such a young girl? Can it last?

That night, as the clock struck ten, her mother retired for the night and her father went into his study to immerse himself in Jewish texts of the Mishnah and the Talmud. Shira took the black, rotary telephone from the hallway, pulled the fifty-foot cord into her room and dialed my phone number. She feared the sound of dialing would be heard outside her room but took the risk anyway.

I was sitting on my couch trying to read court documents and briefs but couldn't concentrate on them, as I eyed my watch and the phone. It finally rang! I immediately picked it up. In a muffled tone, Shira whispered, "Michael, I miss you. I thought about you every moment since I left you. Last weekend seemed like a storybook dream. I wished it had never ended. I'm sorry for talking so much. Tell me about your day. What are you doing?"

My heart was pounding, "I started the day with morning court calls and ended the day with client meetings. I thought about you all day. I want to touch you, feel you and kiss you."

There was silence. Either she didn't know what to say or she was afraid to respond. Regardless, I continued the discussion and asked her to describe her room and what she was wearing. We talked for an hour.

Out of nowhere she blurted out in a whisper, "I miss you too! I can't wait until I see you tomorrow." With that, before I could even say goodnight, I heard the phone click and then a dial tone. I must wait until tomorrow evening when I would be able to smell her sweet essence and touch her soft skin. Was this infatuation, lust or was I actually in love?

The next day, Shira took the graffiti-stained train from Brooklyn, disembarking at the Manhattan subway station. It was a noisy, jerky trip due to the clacking of the train tracks and screeching of grinding wheels filling the car. She was fortunate it wasn't during rush hour when human bodies are crammed together like sardines in a can. The only respite of relief from the heat came from a breeze created by the open windows and the movement of the train.

Shira arrived at my office suite a little before 4 p.m. Pat announced her arrival to me via the office intercom and I rushed to the waiting area to greet her. I briefly introduced Shira to Pat, my office manager.

Pat was a stockily built woman with short, dyed, blonde hair, in her mid-fifties. She had been previously married to an abusive ex-marine, there was nothing my white-collar criminal clients could say to make her blush. She was tough as nails and unafraid to tell my criminal clients to pay their bill on time or they wouldn't get service. She ran the office efficiently, permitting me to concentrate on the practice of criminal law.

I took Shira's left hand and led her into my office. Pat smiled and gave me a funny look. Her curiosity was piqued. Shira was the first girlfriend to visit the office. In her red Keds, she appeared younger than her age. I closed the door, grabbed Shira, passionately kissed her and embraced her like I'd never see her again. Her fiery enthusiastic lips were a godsend. I never craved anyone as I did her, at this moment.

We chose to eat dinner at Ratner's Milk Restaurant on Delancey Street in the Lower East Side in Manhattan. We figured no one from her part of town would travel from Brooklyn to eat there. Entering the restaurant, I immediately caught a whiff of fried cheese and potato blintzes. Our waiter was a man in his fifties who sported a white, short-sleeved shirt and red bow tie. We sat in a booth with wooden benches.

The waiter took our drink order. I had a Coke and Shira ordered a strawberry shake. Shira apologized before we ordered, explaining that her appetite had increased over the past couple of days. We wolfed down Ratner's famous onion rolls with fresh butter and split a side order of cheese blintzes smothered in sour cream. Still hungry, we shared a lox sandwich on an egg bagel with chive cream cheese, a slice of onion and tomato.

As we sat, I placed my hand on top of Shira's hand. She looked around the room to reassure herself that the other patrons were strangers before our fingers intertwined. We talked for hours until it was time to take her home. At night, it wasn't safe for a young girl to take the subway, so we took a Yellow cab to my apartment building, so I could drive her home.

We entered through the garage where I asked the garage attendant's permission to fetch my own car. We walked to it and once there her eyes popped open as she first saw my pride and joy: a 1969, two-door, black Oldsmobile Cutlass 442 with red trim and red leather interior. Shira stood in awe as her hand moved across the smoothly waxed body. "What happened to the van?"

"I borrowed the van from a friend. This is my car."

I opened the passenger door and helped her in as she sat in the bucket seat. There was a roar of the engine as I turned the ignition key. I pressed the button to lower the windows and we drove off. I turned on the FM radio station just as a Simon and Garfunkel song, 'The Sounds of Silence', began to play. As she listened to the words, she said, "How beautiful. The words of their music are so profound?"

"Yes. Some day we will go back to my place and I will play their album for you."

She looked at the dashboard and the various gadgets. "This car is so impressive. It smells new. I have never been in such a fancy automobile. My Aba drives an old Plymouth Fury with four doors. David from the yeshiva had a new car, but after his children ate several times in the back seat the car now smells like food."

"Who's David?"

"He works at the yeshiva in the accounting department for my Aba."

On the ride to Brooklyn, she asked me about the buttons on the door handle. Like a child, she wanted to play with them. She was amazed the windows went up and down with the flick of a switch. "Everyone I know has a window crank. No one has electric car windows." Her words reminded me how young she was.

I parked the car around the corner from her home. A full, bright moon shone in a sky filled with stars. We sat in the car talking. Then we moved toward one another. We embraced and kissed. "Shira, I will see you next week, won't I?" I longed for her in my bed but didn't dare to ask yet.

She slowly got out, stood by my side of the car and

poked her head through the open window. Quietly she whispered, "I have fallen in love with you! I want you to know I miss not sleeping next to you at night."

With that, she turned and ran home like a schoolgirl, leaving me speechless.

Sadly, Shira had to cancel our second date because her mother needed her help. My body was going crazy, I longed to be with her every moment of the day; at night I sought to reach for her. My ability to concentrate on legal matters was hampered by thoughts of making love with her again. I hoped she was feeling the same crazy way. I'd never felt this kind of desire before with anyone. It was amazing.

# Meeting Emah

Two weeks passed. On this night before Shira hung up the telephone, I joked, "If I don't see you soon, I will drive to your place, knock on the front door and tell your parents you are my bashert." She didn't think that was funny and made me promise I wouldn't. The next morning, Shira was running late for her teaching job and failed to return the telephone back to the hallway table before leaving for work.

Emah saw the telephone cord and followed it into Shira's room. She went to retrieve it and return it to the hallway stand. When she lifted the base of the phone off Shira's side table, she discovered a criminal attorney's business card with my name on it: Michael Goldman. Until Emah saw the card, she was not concerned that her daughter's menstrual period was over a week late.

Emah's worst fears played tricks with her mind. Had her daughter been raped, or had she done something where she needed criminal legal advice? Why hadn't Shira told her family that something occurred?

Emah rushed downstairs and took the early morning bus that transported observant Jews who worked in the Diamond District to Midtown Manhattan, a short walking distance from my office. The non-air-conditioned bus was segregated where men and women were not permitted to sit together. The women were required to sit in the back. It started out as a warm day, but for me it would only get hotter.

I had several procedural motions being heard this morning. I was organizing the legal documents in my briefcase when Pat knocked on my door and said, "Mikey." She called me that when clients weren't around. "A Jewish religious woman named Lefkovitz is here to see you. I hope you're not in trouble for cradle-robbing." Then, Pat giggled. I think it was the first time in five years I had seen her laugh at one of her own jokes. I didn't think the joke was funny given the circumstances.

The only Lefkovitz I knew was Shira. Could it be her mother? What would she be doing here? Nervously, I asked, "Pat, would you do me a favor? Ask Max if he is available to handle my motion calls this morning? Tell him it's an emergency. I will grab Mrs. Lefkovitz from the waiting area. Let me know what Max says."

Pat smiled and laughed as she walked down the hall. She was curious, wondering if the lady in the waiting area had something to do with the young girl, she met two weeks earlier.

I took a deep breath. "Mrs. Lefkovitz." I mistakenly offered my hand before remembering she would not touch anyone but her husband. Mrs. Lefkovitz was wearing a wig and what could be

48

mistaken for a housecleaning dress which covered both her knees and elbows. She carried an over-sized cloth purse on her right arm and wore no make-up. "Please, follow me to my office." So, this was the sweet Mom Shira referred to as Emah. To me, she looked tough as nails and she wasn't smiling.

"Did you have an easy time driving into the city? How may I be of service to you?" I asked. She wore an emotionless stone face. Clearly, she was not here to discuss the weather.

She sat down in my office. I offered her coffee or tea, but her raised right hand indicated she did not want anything except words with me. In a pleasant tone I inquired, "What can I do for you today?" I didn't know what to expect.

Just as Mrs. Lefkovitz was about to speak, Pat popped her head into my office. "Don't worry, Max will cover your morning calls. He told me to tell you that you owe him." Then she quickly left, leaving the door ajar, but not before she gave a wicked glance.

Without mincing words, Emah began. "I found your business card by our telephone in my daughter Shira's room. Is my daughter in trouble? Why did she need to call you?"

I moved from behind my desk and sat in the chair next to Mrs. Lefkovitz, leaving plenty of space between us. Her eyes followed me as I moved without blinking. It gave me a second to collect my thoughts. I leaned over and faced her while preparing my answer. "Mrs.

Lefkovitz, though unexpected, I am pleased you are here. I was hoping to have a conversation about Shira and my relationship with her."

Her head quickly swiveled toward me as her eyes grew intense. I had her attention. "Your daughter and I are close friends. I have known her for a little over two weeks though it feels longer." Her mouth opened and before she could say a word, I popped the question. "I want your permission to date your daughter. My intentions are honorable and sincere."

I surprised her as she tried to figure out how I met Shira and why her daughter kept it a secret. She contemplated her next words, as Pat walked in again with a sense of urgency. She said, "I'm sorry for disturbing you, Mr. Goldman, Judge Brown's clerk is on the phone. You must take it!"

"Mrs. Lefkovitz, please excuse me. This shouldn't be more than a minute or two." I picked up the phone. There was no reason to ask Mrs. Lefkovitz to leave the room since she wouldn't hear any privileged client information.

"Michael Goldman speaking… Yes, I understand. But is it possible for my motion to be heard at the end of the call? I can make it there within forty-five minutes. The truth is, I am having a discussion with the rabbi's wife. Stop laughing, it's the truth… Thank you. I will not be late. I'll be leaving this minute."

As I finished the call, Mrs. Lefkovitz had a sense of urgency in her voice when she asked, "Where did you meet my daughter?"

I shook my head and said, "Please ask her."

"Do you love my daughter?"

I was sweating and quite nervous as I choked on the words. I didn't have much experience being asked such questions by a girlfriend's parent. I eyed her as I said, "Yes, I think I love her." I was unsure if she was going to hit or yell at me. Did she view me as an old man chasing after her young daughter? Her eyes had brandished daggers and her face expressed concern.

"Are you Jewish? Do you practice the religion?"

"Yes."

She paused and collected her thoughts. "Come to our house and plan to spend Shabbos with my family. I assume you know our address?" She queried with an arched eyebrow. I nodded my head yes to her question. With that, she thanked me for my honesty and abruptly left, but not before saying, "I see you have more important things to do than sit and talk to me." I wasn't sure how to interpret her words.

I was pretty shaken at this point, but I couldn't afford to indulge my fears. I was late and raced to the courthouse, yet Shira was on my mind. She was expected to visit me that afternoon and I would need to warn her of the conversation I just had. I didn't want her to be blindsided.

# Shira's secret

It had been three weeks since we last had sex. I was hoping tonight we would renew our physical passions in my bed. My mind mapped out a strategy as to how I would get her to my place. I would use the pretense of her mother's visit as the reason we'd have dinner at my apartment. I had to decide if I should tell Shira before or after sex the extent of our conversation.

Unbeknownst to me, Shira had expected but did not get her period. Instead of seeing blood, she experienced swelling of her breasts, an achy body, and a feeling of being nauseous. Having observed her three sisters go through their pregnancies, she was acquainted with the symptoms and was certain she was pregnant, but hoped she was wrong.

When I woke up that morning, I thought it was going to be a glorious day and nothing could go wrong, because I was going to see Shira. Then her mother arrived, and my day went into a tailspin. My mother's favorite expression, "Man plans, and God laughs" roared through my brain.

The elevator delivered Shira to my suite and Pat showed her directly to my office. She appeared exhausted from the train ride. Pat was smirking as Shira

stepped through the doorway. After Pat left, I hurried over to Shira, and kissed her repeatedly as I held her in my arms.

"Shira, I was thinking we would have dinner at my place. I have things to discuss with you and not in kosher restaurants which have ears."

"I would like that. I have things that I need to tell you too. What's on tonight's menu? I'm starved."

The cab ride to my place wasn't that bad considering that in Manhattan, the rush hour can last two hours..

Shira was deep in thought as the taxi meter clicked. There was something on her mind. I couldn't put my finger on it. Her smile seemed tarnished. Something was troubling her. She held my hand tightly to reassure me as I started a conversation.

"I had a visitor today." I paused for a few moments and waited to pique her curiosity before I continued. "Your mother."

Her head jerked, jaw dropped, and her eyes popped opened. I had her undivided attention. She was her mother's daughter in the way she physically responded. "What did she want? How did she know about you?"

"It seems, she found my business card next to the telephone in your bedroom this morning."

"Ah, I'm so stupid. I was in such a rush, I forgot to return the phone to the hallway table." She put her hand on her forehead and eagerly asked, "What did Emah say?"

I was about to tell her, when the cab stopped, and the driver asked for five dollars and fifty cents. I gave him an extra dollar tip and we exited the cab in front of my apartment building.

The doorman nodded as we stepped from the vehicle. "Good afternoon, Mr. Goldman."

"Good afternoon, Roger."

Like a curious child, her head rotated as she noticed and observed every detail in the green carpeted lobby. She found the beautifully decorated ground floor and hanging crystal chandeliers like a storybook description.

We entered the elevator, and I pressed the button for the tenth floor. Shira noted the elevator's interior was painted with a shiny gold finish. Looking up, she saw her reflection in the mirrored ceiling and glowed with amazement.

The elevator doors opened. We walked to my corner unit. She looked for and spotted the mezuzah on the door frame. She traditionally kissed her fingers after touching it.

I opened the door and permitted her the honor of being the first to enter. I placed my keys on the edge of the kitchen counter, offered her a stool and asked, "Shira, may I offer you some wine? Would you prefer white or red?"

"Not right now. Maybe glass of water. Tell me what did Emah have to say?" All the while her eyes took in my furnishings, the art and the panoramic view of New

York's skyline.

"Do you mind if I talk and cook at the same time?" I started to roll up my sleeves while pulling pots and pans out of the cabinet.

"Only if you permit me to assist you in the kitchen."

I motioned for her to join me, as I first washed my hands and then ran water from the faucet into a pot. Pointing, I said, "These drawers and cabinets to the left of the stove are all my meat utensils, dishes and cookware. Everything to the right is milk."

"What are we having for dinner?"

"Pasta with cooked vegetables in an olio sauce. Does that meet with your approval?" A smiling nod of her head said yes.

I handed her the garlic, onions and mushrooms. To my surprise, she took the flat edge of the knife to crack the outer shell of the garlic and then expertly minced it. She adroitly sliced the onions and the mushrooms as I turned on the burners. I placed salt and a couple of drops of olive oil in the water and waited for it to boil. She asked for butter to sauté the veggies.

Shira opened my refrigerator for the butter, perhaps scanning the contents to see how kosher I kept my kitchen. I think I passed the test based on her facial expression.

I grabbed the plates and glasses to set the table and continued. "Your mother loves you very much; otherwise, she would not have come to my office. She wanted to know about us. I refused to answer her when

she asked how we met. Instead, I told her I love you and I wanted her permission to date you."

Shira initially froze waiting for me to continue. "Your Mom had tons of questions for me but didn't get to ask them because I had to run to court." Shira began to cry and covered her eyes with her hands. "Don't cry yet. Your mother is expecting you to tell her about us tonight when you get home. My advice is to tell her the whole truth. Remember, none of this was your fault."

As she started to speak, the tears flowed like a river. "Michael, should I tell her that I may be pregnant?"

In shock, I dropped the pasta box on the counter and placed my hand to cover my opened mouth. She had caught me by surprise. I needed time to collect my thoughts and evaluate what I wanted with my future. What were the ramifications? Marriage? Was I ready for marriage? How would I break the news to my Mom that I was getting married to my pregnant teenage girlfriend? How would I tell my friends? What about her parents? Oh shit!

When I said nothing, she began biting on her thumb nail and held her breath. She was anxious fearing my response and possible rejection.

The few moments it took me to respond must have felt like an eternity to her. The only sounds came from the boiling pasta water and sizzling vegetables in the frypan as she waited for my answer. "Shira, in the brief time we have known each other, I have fallen in love with you. You are the one I think about when I rise in

the morning and at night when I close my eyes. I wasn't expecting to get married or have a child anytime soon."

Shira looked as she was going to cry as I continued, "I want to marry you! I would not be truthful if I didn't say you caught me off guard tonight. I guess we are going to have a child." Her eyes sparkled and tears of joy replaced the fear. I walked over to give her a reassuring hug. Inside, I was sweating and had the beginning of a panic attack as I started to consider all the repercussions of my commitment.

Somewhat relieved, no longer holding her breath, she still needed to ask, "You're not saying that just because I'm pregnant? Are you?" Her sad eyes waited for a reply.

"No, you are the first girl I have ever been in love with. Besides, our child will need two loving parents." We held each other until the smell of burning vegetables called us into the kitchen.

We ate a delicious pasta dinner and had a dish of Neapolitan ice cream for dessert, at which point we began discussing our future as I drank a glass of wine.

"I forgot to tell you that your Mom invited me to spend this Shabbos at your home." Shira was both surprised and worried how her father would react. This would be the first time that a marital suitor was invited to spend the holiday before there was an engagement.

"I want to ask your father for your hand in marriage sometime over Shabbos. Do you have a problem with that?" She shook her head no, but I could tell by her facial expression she feared her father's answer.

"I think for the sake of your community and your family, we should get married in the next two to three weeks." She smiled and agreed. She stood up and gave me a big hug as happy tears slipped down her cheeks. I could tell from her the gleam in her eyes that an enormous emotional burden had been lifted from her shoulders. It had been now transferred to mine.

"Will you be comfortable living and raising our family here in Manhattan? I have three bedrooms with — plenty of room for one or two kids."

"I will be wherever you are. My heart will follow you forever. You will need to show me around the neighborhood and point out if there are kosher butchers, restaurants and shuls close by?"

"Yes, plenty. That's not a problem."

She looked at her watch; it was half past six. Shira said, "Show me around the apartment where we will be living."

I stood up and we started to walk around my unit after she first used the guest bathroom. It gave me a moment to take a deep breath which allowed my heartbeat return to normal and reflect on our future.

I started the tour. "The kitchen has the attached eating area here. Around the corner is the living room and down the hall there are two bathrooms and three bedrooms. The master bedroom has the third attached bathroom."

Emphatically she said, "Show me my new

bedroom." With all tonight's revelations I had forgotten about having sex.

I opened the door and pointed out the queen-sized bed, the dressers and the two separate closets. I turned to show her the master bathroom. I thought she was behind me. I looked back and she wasn't there. From the corner of my eye, I spied her taking off her clothes under the bedsheet.

"Michael, please turn off the light and join me."

She took the words out of my mouth. I was speechless. I tossed my clothes on the floor and jumped into the bed alongside her. Our fingers investigated the contours of each other's bodies, as if it were the first time as we passionately kissed. Our legs intertwined like puzzle pieces coming together. When the breathless excitement reached a fever pitch, we made love. Instinctively, she knew what to do. For me, it was earth-shattering evening as I melted into her and we became one.

Afterwards, we talked about the baby and possible names. She pressed the point and made me promise that our children must attend Jewish Day School. Then, Shira provided me with ideas on how I should approach her father over Shabbos.

We showered and for the first time enjoyed the unique experience washing each other. "It feels so strange having you wash me. I enjoy it." She had lost her inhibitions of being naked and became addicted to showing me her expressions of love. Before we left the apartment, I called downstairs and asked the garage attendant to ready my car.

In the elevator we kissed as we descended and once reaching the lobby, we walked hand-in-hand into the garage where my car awaited us with the engine running.

Once in the car, I looked over to her and said, "Shira, I was surprised that you initiated lovemaking. Don't get me wrong, it was incredible, and I secretly hoped it would happen. What made you decide to go for it?"

Embarrassed she blushed and giggled before saying, "Michael, I have those feelings and desires that you have. I've craved your touch and the warmth of your body next to mine. I am pregnant. There is nothing I can do to change the past. Sadly, I don't have any memories of that evening when we first made love. At home, in bed, I closed my eyes wishing I could relive that experience with you when we conceived our child. After you agreed to marry me, I thought, why not? This is the man who I am destined to be with all the days of my life, my bashert. Why wait any longer?"

Her face continued to blush as she said, "Making love to you was better than I could have ever imagined. Even better than the fantasy in my trash novels. You are the lover that one only dreams about having." With that she covered her face. As I listened to her words, I understood the difference making love with her and the sex I had with countless others. I concentrated on her satisfaction before mine and in doing so, reaped personal rewards.

Every conversation we had, reinforced my decision that I had chosen to marry the right girl. We had found that we had much in common including family values. I had a sense that she would be there for me in the best and worst of times and become my trusted best friend.

In the car, I tempted fate by making future plans with Shira to visit the city clerk's office Friday and apply for a marriage license before driving to her parent's place where I would ask her father for his blessing. I realized that some time tonight I had to call my Mom to let her know I was serious with someone and we would be planning a wedding in the coming weeks. I almost feared Mom's reaction as much as Shira's father.

I parked several houses away from her parents' residence. Before she left my vehicle and faced her own moment of truth, I wanted her to know that starting a family didn't mean she had to surrender her dreams. "I want you to pursue your college degree in teaching, literature or English. I think it's important. Between our parents, babysitters and daycare we will make it work so you can attend classes. The City College isn't far from our condo by bus."

She leaned over, hugged and kissed me. "You are my future and my life. I will always love you! When the time comes, I'm sure God will find a way for me to pursue my educational aspirations. Thank you for considering my needs, not many men would."

As Shira entered her parents' apartment building and crept up the stairs at a deliberate pace, she contemplated what she would say to her mother. She feared opening the door and confronting the unknown — the moment of truth. She turned the front door handle and slowly stepped inside turning her head in all direction in search for her Mom.

She found Emah waiting in a chair facing her. A single light remained lit behind her. The apartment was otherwise dark and quiet. Before Emah said a word, Shira said, "Forgive me for not telling you. Will you ever forgive me? I want to tell you everything that happened to me and my future plans."

Emah pointed with her index finger. "Let's go to your room. I want to hear everything and then I will pass judgment."

"Emah, promise me you will not get angry until I finish telling you the entire story. There is so much to tell. Some of it will be difficult for me to share." Emah agreed. They walked into Shira's room and closed the door. Emah stood with her arms crossed as Shira sat on her bed. Shira's eyes faced the ground and Emah's face lacked any emotional expression.

Shira had her hands in her lap as she spoke in a whisper. "Emah, my girlfriend lied to me and tricked me about the sleeping arrangements last month in the Catskills. She wanted me to share a tent with her and two men. I was angry and demanded that she take me home. At that point she gave me a pill to calm down promising that after I was relaxed, she'd take me a proper place for Shabbos The pill is a drug known as LSD, Michael said it is also known as a hallucinogenic drug." Emah shook her head.

"Michael found me crying on the wet ground, hungry and lost. Out of the kindness of his heart he offered me a place to stay in his van and fed me. The drug caused me to lose my inhibitions and believe that I was married." Hesitating and embarrassed, Shira lowered her voice to a whisper.

"The drug caused me to freely perform wedding night nuptials. I was shocked when I woke the next morning naked under his sheet." Shira covered her face with her hands as her eyes watered.

Her mother was shocked by the revelation. She covered her mouth as sadness gripped her soul. "Emah, Michael didn't know I was drugged or a virgin when he made love to me." She took a deep breath before continuing. "Michael and I stayed together for the next two days in his van sleeping on an air mattress. He fed and clothed me. Once I told him the kind of girl I was, we didn't have sex again that weekend. We have talked on the telephone almost every night and we had dinner tonight and two weeks ago."

Scared, and at the same time relieved, Shira knew the truth left her exposed to having shamed her family. She took a deep breath knowing that the next revelation would be the toughest. "Please forgive me. I should have told you the truth, but I was afraid of the embarrassment I caused the family. I lied when I told you I was at the library and that was wrong."

Shira paused, closed her eyes and said a quick prayer before continuing. "Emah, I think I am pregnant." Her mother gasped. "Michael plans to ask Aba over Shabbos if he will bless our marriage. He wants us to get married in the next two to three weeks. On Friday, we plan to get a marriage license. Now you know everything. There is nothing else that I have not told you."

Emah walked towards the bed and hugged her daughter as together they wept. Emah finally broke the silence. "I wish you had come and told me. I love you. I will support you because you told me the truth and pray for your happiness. I must tell your father, in my way and at the right time. Say nothing to no one. Not even your sisters." Shira was happy to agree.

Emah thought for a second and felt compelled to share her heartfelt emotions. "I am not going to lie to you. I wish you would be marrying one of the religious boys from the neighborhood. It pains me you are unmarried and pregnant. Thankfully, Michael appears honorable. I will pray your marriage is a good one and you will be happy all the days of your life."

"Emah, thank you. I promise I will never shame you and Aba again."

"Do you love him? Do you believe in your heart he will be a loving and religiously observant husband?"

Shira's eyes sparkled as she smiled and said, "Emah, I love him with all my soul and all my heart. I don't know exactly how observant he is, but he has a righteous soul."

"Where will you live? Have you discussed what life will be like once there is a child in your lives?"

"Michael has a three-bedroom condominium in Manhattan. He says there are shuls, butchers and restaurants in the area. He already keeps kosher. He wants me to be the decision-maker on our religious lifestyle and which Jewish day school to send our children. He said that he will accept my decisions."

"Do you know I met with him today at his office?"

"Yes, Michael told me. What did you think of him?"

"I think he loves you. You had better go to bed because you need to get up early for work. Besides a girl in your condition must have her rest." Shira changed into a cotton nightgown, Emah kissed her forehead and turned off the overhead light before Shira said her evening prayers.

The euphoric roller coaster of emotions quickly dissipated on my way home. The harsh reality of the lifetime and financial commitment now weighed on me. I promised myself, once back at my place I must call Mom. She'll think I'm crazy or on drugs, I thought, when I tell her of my upcoming nuptials to a black hatter's daughter that I have known less than a month.

"Mom, I hope I didn't wake you. Is this a good time

to talk?"

She yawned. "I was watching the evening news. It's always a good time to hear from you. Is there something on your mind? You usually don't call at this late hour." I asked if she was sitting down, and I told her my news.

Raising her voice, she said, "What! An ultra-religious rabbi's daughter? Do you know what you are getting into? They don't live in the same world that you grew up in and know so well. I hope she isn't sixteen."

"She's almost eighteen."

"OMG Michael, you're robbing the cradle. Next she'll tell you she won't use birth control during the marriage."

"Between us, she's pregnant. More importantly, I love her more than anyone I have ever known."

"Oh my God! I don't know what to say." She stuttered, looking for the words before saying, "I want to meet her." I thought Mom was going to faint.

"I will bring her by, on Saturday night probably after nine-thirty. Don't let her know what I told you and don't tell my sister or anyone that she is pregnant."

"Don't worry. I'll pray for your happiness. I thought you were the most sensible of my two children. Now I may need to reconsider that."

That sleepless night my brain tried to make sense of everything that had transpired that day. All I could think of was someone in the heavens was having a good laugh at my expense.

# Shabbos with her family

We arrived at City Hall during a large anti-Vietnam war protest. We had to circumvent the barricades erected in front of the building. The crowds were noisy, and obscenities were hurled by hundreds of rioters at the police. The police wore hard, blue riot helmets, and held batons in their hands while they jockeyed with the protesters for control of the streets. Both the police and protesters had bullhorns, making it impossible to understand what anyone was saying. Adding to the mayhem were blaring car horns, a testament of the drivers' frustration as they were denied access to the intersection.

After securing our marriage license, I pulled up in front of Shira's parents' building. Shira handed me a black kippah she had crocheted for me. It must have taken her the better part of a week. Saying, "I wanted to give you a small gift to say thank you for everything. I love you."

Upon seeing Shira in my car, her nephews removed metal garbage cans and a broom that was used to reserve the parking space in front of her building. Brooklyn was a different world from what I was used to.

There was a slew of religious kids waiting for us. I

found out that they all were her nephews and nieces. The girls were attired in their Shabbos dresses and tights, and wore their long hair pulled back. The boys wore button-down dress shirts and kippahs, and their tzitzits hung out over the front pockets of their trousers. When they noticed Shira, all the children waved and approached her with hugs. A couple of kids raced upstairs to announce our arrival.

I opened the car door for Shira and together we walked into the building. I had my overnight bag slung over my right shoulder. Several of the children followed us up the stairs, vying for Shira's attention. I wanted one last kiss for luck, but with an audience that was impossible. There was no reason to hide our relationship, but I had to observe the local custom of no touching in this foreign land of Brooklyn.

I knew the next twenty-five hours would be challenging. I was not the yeshiva student Shira's family would have chosen. I was entering a world to which I was unaccustomed and for which I was unprepared. I felt immense guilt because Shira was unmarried and pregnant. I maintained no regret that I loved her and desired her hand in marriage. All these thoughts whirled through my mind as we approached the apartment door entrance.

If that wasn't enough, I grew apprehensive as I imagined her father's reaction when confronted with the news. A voice inside me said, you can still retreat home before sundown. I ignored the inner voice and decided to face my fears. Besides, killing and maiming are violations of the Sabbath, so that somewhat limited her father's -choice of responses. I must be on my guard for questions that could expose the illicit relationship I had with Shira in front of her extended family. I did not want to bring shame to her.

I considered myself religious; however, my religious observances were less rigid and not on par with her family's practice. I cooked on Shabbos, used the elevator and I did other things strictly forbidden in her world.

As we walked up the stairs, in the dark, narrow corridor to the second floor of the three-story brownstone, we saw Shira's mom waiting for us with a warm inviting smile. She was dressed in a stylish, yet modest, blue dress. Her hair was styled, and she wore make-up. She appeared more composed than when we last met at my office. "Mrs. Lefkovitz, thank you for the invitation. Please accept these small gifts." I had brought flowers and a bottle of red kosher wine.

She smiled as I handed her the gifts. "Michael, the flowers are beautiful. You are a welcome guest. I hope you enjoy Shabbos with us. I would appreciate it if you would call me Emah. I feel you are like a member of the family. Take your bag and place it on the side of the couch over there."

Her hand directed me there. "You will sleep in the living room." Lowering her voice, she continued. "You'll sleep on the air mattress tonight. I am told you have experience sleeping on them. Unfortunately, for you, you will not have to share it with anyone we know."

I nervously chuckled. Shira was flabbergasted and could not believe what came out of her mother's mouth. Eventually, Shira smiled. Her mother's discreet joke eased my nerves a tad. The women walked over to the mahogany buffet table, where a slew of candles and candle holders had been prearranged.

The dining room table with multiple leaves extended into the living room. All the regulars were expected for dinner according to Shira: Shira's siblings, their spouses and children plus two unrelated yeshiva students. The total number of Shabbos guests appeared to be twenty-five. The table was set with fine china, crystal salt and pepper shakers, white cloth napkins and a white tablecloth.

The women proceeded to light the Shabbos candles. They covered their eyes and prayed for their families. They recited the blessings and at the same time put the backs of their hands toward the candles and then brought theirs hands closer to their faces. They repeated this exercise three times as they reached out to guide the essence of the candles' spirit toward them.

Afterwards, Shira whispered, "Michael, I have included you in my prayers." My instinct, and the tradition in my Mom's home, was for me to hug and kiss her. I wished everyone "Good Shabbos" and puckered my lips as I drew close enough to kiss Shira, until her eyes opened wide and she shook her head, signaling, do not kiss me. She reminded me where we were.

Shira's father, known as the Rav, along with her brothers and brothers-in-law appeared and entered through the front door all at once. I heard the Rav's jovial voice as he shouted, "Good Shabbos" to everyone in the room. He wore a traditional black suit, black overcoat, a white button-down shirt and a black top hat. His long, gray beard was neatly trimmed. His thinning gray hair peeked out once he discarded the top hat for a large black knit kippah. The Rav had the physical appearance of Santa Claus, with a little less abdominal padding.

After they took off their coats, each of the fathers put their hands over their respective children's heads and individually blessed them. Then, they kissed their wives."

The Rav walked over to the dining room. Everyone followed and took their assigned places around the table. I felt conspicuous by my appearance I was the only male without payos dangling in front of his ear lobes and the only male over eighteen who didn't sport a beard.

Emah instructed me to sit in the seat to the right of the Rav. She sat in the seat to his immediate left, closest to the kitchen door. Shira was at the other end of the table, far away from me. I'm sure Shira's parents intentionally planned it that way.

The Rav looked at me. "Michael, it is my pleasure

to have you as our guest. Thank you for accepting my wife's invitation and spending this Shabbos with us." Then, he asked if I knew what it meant to be married.

I looked at him and wasn't sure how to answer, but quickly found my voice. "Sir, marriage is a solemn commitment between a man and a woman to love one another all the days of their lives." What else was I going to say to my future father-in-law? Shira tried to listen, but the side conversations made it impossible.

"It's said when God created the world, he created man and woman. Yet, later in the first chapter of Genesis, it states that God created Eve. So, what is meant when we say God created man and woman before God created Eve?" the Rav inquired.

"I'm not sure."

"When God initially created man, the male and female were a single flame that burned together; they were one being. They separated into two beings as they acquired human form. When they grew separate in thought and deed dreadful things happened, like the eating of the forbidden fruit. When two young people get married, they should always be united like a flame and remain inseparable."

After the Rav finished his comments, everyone joined in singing two traditional Friday night Hebrew blessings. Afterward, the Rav recited the kiddush, sanctification of the Sabbath with wine.

Everyone walked into the kitchen. Those wearing jewelry removed the items from their fingers and each took turns ritually washing their hands. We returned to the table in silence. The Rav threw coarse salt on the two challah loaves, held them in the air and said the blessing over the bread, after which we all responded, "Amen," acknowledging our thankfulness to God for the meal that we were about to eat. Rav then distributed pieces of the blessed loaf to each of us to eat. As soon as the participants consumed their piece of challah, they immediately started talking.

The children passed out bowls of chicken matzah ball soup. The most pleasing smell of fresh chicken soup quickly filtered into my nostrils and conjured up those vivid memories of my family's Shabbos dinners before my grandfather passed away. The aroma whetted my appetite, and I couldn't wait to dip my soup spoon into the bowl in front of me.

As my spoon reached for the bowl, the Rav began to ask me more questions. "I hear you are a lawyer and have become a close friend of my daughter."

"Yes, sir."

"Do you love and honor your parents and when did you last visit with them?"

"My father passed away over a year ago. My Mom and I are close. We talk at least three times a week and we go out for dinner as often as we can."

"May your father's name always be remembered, as a blessing. Do you have siblings? What is your relationship with them?" He asked me questions in rapid fire succession and he consumed his soup as he listened to my responses.

"I have a sister. We are a close family. We try to spend religious and secular holidays together."

The Rav asked these questions, leaving little if any time to consume more than one spoonful between answers. When it was time for the main course, the children gathered the bowls and brought them back to the kitchen. A child grabbed my bowl just as my spoon was reaching for it, but not before I could enjoy another taste.

The main course was served while I was still being skillfully interrogated. The entire table listened to my answers while they continued to eat. I was this evening's entertainment. I felt like I was on the witness stand and an opposing attorney was drilling me with questions, hoping to uncover my hidden secrets.

"I hear you want to spend time and date my youngest daughter. Why do you believe I should permit her to do so?"

"Rav, with all due respect, I believe there has been a mistake." He stopped eating and shifted his eyes to watch my lips. "I do not want to date your daughter." Everyone seemed shocked. I could hear a sharp intake of Emah's breath. They all stopped eating, mouths and eyes trained on me, waiting for my next utterance. Even Shira was nervous.

"Rav, I want your permission to marry your youngest daughter. I'm not worthy of her. You and your wife have raised a lovely, bright, articulate and ethically high-minded person. I hope that I will become worthy of her."

With that said, I paused, caught my breath and added, "I will spend all the days of my life loving and caring for her and our children."

The Rav almost choked. Everyone looked at Shira for her reaction. She smiled and looked overjoyed. The Rav cleared his throat and said, "We shouldn't discuss marriage at the Shabbos dinner table." He abruptly changed gears. "Michael, my wife and daughter cooked a wonderful Shabbos dinner, and your plate is empty. We will talk tomorrow. Pass the chicken and rice to this young man. You must eat. Tomorrow we will talk." My forehead and my armpits were dripping with sweat from the encounter. I recall thinking that I could use a Seagram's straight up, right about now.

After dinner, the Rav quietly asked me to join him in the morning as he walked to shul. Twenty minutes later, the lights in the dining room and living room turned off automatically thanks to preset electrical timers.

I was still nervous and shaking as I washed my face after dinner. A little voice asked: could I live in her world, even for a weekend? Without answering the inner voice, I quietly returned to my 'bed'.

Shira sneaked out of her bedroom and whispered in my ear without waking the students on the couch beside me. "I love you. You were wonderful tonight. Sweet dreams." She gave me a loving French kiss before tiptoeing back to her room.

The next morning, the Rav was ready for me. We each grabbed a piece of sweet coffee cake for breakfast and drank a cup of coffee. "Young man, did you sleep well? Are you ready to leave for shul?"

"Thank you for asking. Yes, whenever you are ready, sir."

We proceeded down the stairs and onto the street. The morning was cooler, yet the leaves were still green. There was no trace of the coming fall season in the flora. There was no traffic on his street and the only sounds I heard came from birds and airplanes.

He was the first to start the conversation. "If I were willing to consent to your marriage, will I be losing a daughter? Family is important to me and obviously you can't walk from your apartment to ours. How will you two maintain a relationship with my family, and is it important to you?"

"Rav, your daughter and your wife will work out holiday schedules as to when we will stay here with you in Brooklyn. I have encouraged Shira to enroll in college. If God provides us with a child, I will ask Emah and my mother to babysit and help raise our child. In doing so, I would hope to create a special bond between our child and its grandparents. I will always speak of you and your family with honor and encourage a bond between my children and their cousins."

His serious tone underscored his feelings. "I understand you want to marry in the next couple of weeks. I'm not comfortable with this situation. As a parent who loves his daughter, a devoutly religious young woman, I am shocked and dismayed by the unfolding of these events. I am quite disturbed my daughter is in the condition she's in, yet I am left with few alternatives."

As we talked, his hands were clenched behind his back and he moved side to side at a slow pace with his head bowed towards the ground. He wanted to speak freely and openly without being overheard. "Now that I have spoken my piece, have you given thought to the wedding day?"

"Yes sir. We have chosen September eighteenth. It's a Thursday. Eighteen is a lucky Jewish number." I felt the worst was over; we were going to get his blessing. I started to notice my surroundings. My heart could now beat normally as my worst fears were arrested.

Rav cleared his throat. "Today is August thirtieth. Rosh Hashanah begins on September thirteenth and Yom Kippur begins on Sunday night the twenty-first. It is quite unusual to have a wedding during the solemn days of reflection between the two holidays. Can't you wait until after Yom Kippur?"

"It is my understanding; Jewish law states a pregnant woman may not be required to fast during Yom Kippur if it would endanger the fetus. If Shira was theoretically pregnant, she might be compelled to drink and eat. Her sisters and sisters-in-law would observe her eating and would know she is pregnant. Shira's reputation would be ruined. If we were married, we would spend Yom Kippur at my residence. No one would see her if she needed to eat or drink."

"Hmm. You must be an accomplished lawyer. You researched and prepared for my questions in advance. Hundreds of people will want to attend this wedding from the neighborhood, our extended family, the shul, the yeshiva and people outside the religious community. How can we explain the rush to get married and the unusual timing?"

"What if I was worried that a family member had health issues and we chose to marry now rather than in a year's time, so that person could attend the wedding?"

"Is that true? Is someone ill?"

"Sir, I didn't say someone was ill, only I was worried that there was a health issue. Rav, we would be honored if you would perform the ceremony."

This time, he cleared his throat twice, as he looked at me and smiled. "You are a wise man. The wedding will be here at my shul on the afternoon of the eighteenth. It will be my honor to officiate. It will be necessary to announce the wedding date at the shul today. Is that acceptable?"

"Yes, sir."

"Are you familiar with the aufruf ceremony? It is the celebration on Shabbos before the wedding where I'll bless your upcoming union. I will schedule it for next Shabbos, September seventh. We can't have it on

Rosh Hashanah. Can you read the Haftorah, next week?"

The Haftorah was a Hebraic reading of the prophets. I replied, "Rav, I wish I had the skill to prepare and read it in a week's time, but I don't have the ability to do it."

"Don't worry, one of my sons will read it. I will take care of the logistics for the aufruf."

We entered the Rav's orthodox shul. It was an old, dark, stone structure. The men bowed their heads, and some tipped their hats to show respect as they greeted the Rav with the words, "Good Shabbos, Rav." Shira's father took his place in front of the congregation on the bimah in his designated high-backed, brown leather chair.

I placed the white tallis with two long black stripes around my shoulders and walked down the aisle of the sanctuary. Being a stranger, I received curious glances from the other men. It was my tradition to wear a tallis. I was later told that in this shul only married men wore them. The unmarried mostly wore black suits, and smaller version of the tallis under their white outer button-down dress shirts.

Some men were studying texts or saying prayers before the formal call to prayer was sounded. Others walked around and participated in casual conversations, broaching assorted topics including, but not limited to the weather, how the Mets were doing and how the Cubs had too much of a lead for the Mets to catch up. Several of the old-timers lamented that they missed the Dodgers. The older ones conversed in Yiddish while the younger ones spoke mostly in English.

The sanctuary was divided into men and women's sections with a four-foot-high dividing wall separating the two sections. The rows of seating were made of dated, worn, oak wood pews. There must have been thirty rows of seating in each section. In front of each seat there was a shelf containing a siddur and a Tanakh to read during the service. The Torahs were contained in a tall, dark, walnut wood structure known as the 'aron' or ark in English. It stood in the front and middle of the sanctuary where the men and women faced. The 'eternal light' hung from the top of the Ark. The initials for the Ten Commandments were carved on the Ark's walnut outer doors.

Stained glass windows depicting biblical stories, were etched on the windows on the north and south sides of the building. Over twenty antique hanging lights illuminated the sanctuary. There were dark areas in need of replacement bulbs. The vaulted ceiling must have been thirty-five feet high at its apex.

I saw a couple of hands waving which got my attention. I realized they were the Rav's sons, inviting me to join them. They wanted me to feel part of the family, knowing I would be marrying their sister in the near future. Yeshmel handed me a siddur and welcomed me, just as the service was beginning.

Sitting with the family and walking in with the Rav

had raised the attention of the congregants in the shul. They noticed that I was clean shaven, and my non-conforming manner of dress marked me as an outsider. That sparked questions why I was sitting with the Lefkovitz family.

During the service, I noticed men pulling at the shirts, arms or tallits of Shira's brothers. I knew they were talking about me because I heard Shira's name being mentioned.

The questioners would nod their heads up and down and walk away. I watched out of the corner of my eye as the conversation spread like wildfire as others, pointed in my direction. I was the topic of hot gossip. I knew gossiping is a forbidden sin in Jewish law and I was amused to be the center of it.

Some attendees chatted loudly requiring the Rav to hit his fist on the wooden table in front of him seeking to silence the needless chatter. Microphones were not permitted on Shabbos, adding to the difficulty of hearing the prayer leader when the volume of chitchatting increased. Unfortunately, the Rav's warning was only a temporary fix to silencing the idle prattling.

After services, many came up to me, introduced themselves, wished me a mazel tov as they unsuccessfully tried to invade my privacy by asking personal questions.

After shul I returned to the Lefkovitz residence and ate a hearty meal with the family. After lunch, I took delight watching Rav on the carpet, playing with his grandchildren. Looking at him now, on the floor, he appeared as a big teddy bear rather than an imposing figure. Little would one expect this dignified, well-respected scholar enjoyed his grandchildren more than studying his books on Shabbos. One by one, everyone in the apartment went to take a traditional Shabbos day nap — some in beds, others in chairs and couches.

Emah had told Shira after seeing me standing by myself that she wasn't needed in the kitchen. Emah gave Shira permission to take a stroll around the neighborhood with me where I shared my conversation that I had with her father. She shared the conversations she had with her mother.

"Michael, Emah consented to my spending time next Wednesday with you, but I must be home early enough to get a restful night's sleep, so I can report to work the following day. She told me that she agrees with me that you will be a fine husband."

With excitement I said, "Awesome. Wednesday, we can shop for a ring! Okay?"

She broke into a huge smile. The joy on her face glowed like a campfire. "Yes, I can't wait. Michael, you do know that the wedding ring needs to be made of solid metal with no stones or breaks? You will also need to purchase a kittel, to wear during the ceremony."

I was a little lost. "Why would I need to wear a kittel? At my shul, all the men get married in tuxedos or suits. I thought kittels were only worn by the dead and

82

by men on the high holidays?"

"It's the custom at our shul for the groom to wear a kittel over their suit during the wedding ceremony in Brooklyn. Some wear it after the ceremony too. Jewish folklore says the groom and his kallah, you know, the bride, are innocent and holy on their wedding day. Satan will seek to do them ill-will. The groom dresses in his kittel as if it's a burial to fool Satan."

"Shira, you don't believe in these superstitions, do you?" Just then I sneaked a kiss. She quickly looked around, saw no one, ignored protocols and gave me a quick, but passionate kiss in return.

As we strolled, our fingers brushed against one another. I confessed, "I was apprehensive coming here this weekend. I feared your father's reaction and I was afraid of the unknown. Your father and mother have gone out of their way to show me kindness. I have discovered a profound appreciation for their lifestyle that I would never had known except for you."

"It means a lot that you love my family. For better or worse our union will be stronger because of family relationships."

"Sorry to change the subject, but speaking of families, tonight, after Shabbos, will your parents permit you to come with me to my Mom's home to announce our wedding plans? I told her about us, and she wants to meet you. Don't be surprised if my sister is there too."

"I would be honored to meet your family tonight."

"I was thinking that maybe we should tell my mom what to expect as far the wedding formalities and what's expected of her. I'm sure Mom will say she has nothing to wear and there's very little time to have a new dress made."

Shira laughed. "Michael, you just don't understand. Women find these things important, especially what she will wear to her son's wedding. Yes, I will explain everything."

That evening, we arrived at my Mom's home on Long Island. It was close to 10 p.m. We pulled into her circular driveway. I sensed Shira felt nervous as I knocked on the door. She barely spoke on the hour plus drive to Mom's place. My mother appeared, smartly dressed in a colorful skirt, wide-collared white shirt and a single diamond pendant necklace.

We entered the house and before I could introduce Shira, my mother said, "No need Michael." She walked over to Shira, hugged her and said, "Shira, please call me Barbara or call me Mom, whatever makes you feel comfortable." Relieved, Shira immediately smiled as she felt my mother's genuine warmth. They walked into the kitchen.

In the kitchen, Carol hugged Shira. "I'm Michael's older sister. I'm sorry my husband couldn't be here to meet you, but he is babysitting our two kids."

Mom was nervous knowing Shira was religious and wanted to make a good impression by showing Shira that the food items were kosher. Shira felt uneasy and politely said, "Please, Barbara, it's not necessary. I trust you." After that, they both relaxed. The women came out of the kitchen with a tray of food and drinks. Mom provided enough refreshments for an army.

Mom then proceeded to embarrass me by retrieving photo albums of my childhood. Carol told Shira how she helped bathe me when I was an infant. Yes, there were black and white date-stamped baby pictures of me naked in the tub with soap bubbles in my hair. Other embarrassing photographs included me on the changing table.

Shira laughed and commented, "You were adorable, and you had pudgy cheeks."

Mom took a breath and said, "Shira, I have not attended an ultra-orthodox wedding since I was a young girl. As the mother of the groom, will you help me figure out what I should be doing and what to expect?"

"I'd be honored. The first part of the wedding ceremony usually begins at 4:00 p.m. It's called kabbalat panim. I am hoping our families will arrive at two-ish for pictures, so we can take family photos before the ceremony. Michael, remind me that we must arrange to call a photographer."

Carol said, "If you need a suggestion, I have the name and number of the guy we used, he's very good and reasonable."

"Great. Michael, will you get the information from your sister?" I nodded yes.

"Shira, remind me, what is the kabbalat panim

ceremony?"

"The kabbalat panim is where I sit on a chair of honor along with you and my mom on either side of me. We will greet the female guests and enjoy refreshments. Your son will be in another room with the men, including my male family members, where they drink scotch and wine and sing songs. The gathering of the men is a called a tisch. The tisch should last forty-five minutes or so.

"After the tisch, Michael will walk over to the women's room where I will be waiting. Accompanying him will be a trail of men walking behind him and singing. Michael will put the veil over my face. By doing so he is making a commitment to clothe and protect me." Shira sipped the ice-cold lemonade from her glass before continuing.

"What's next?" asked my mom.

"Then, all the attendees will go into the sanctuary for the ceremony. The women will sit on the left side of the aisle and the men on the right side. Once everyone is seated, the music will play and the wedding party, consisting of our immediate families, will walk down the aisle. Eventually, Michael and I will be under the chuppah. My father will be officiating the ceremony."

Carol recalled her wedding at that moment. "The rabbi told us that when I circled my husband seven times, our souls would join as one. What I loved was the idea we were no longer dedicating ourselves to our individual needs and lives. Rather, we were now dedicating ourselves to each other. Only by wanting the best for one another would we truly find happiness in our marriage."

Shira's face lit up. "Wow, Carol, that was beautiful. I will remember that when I circle Michael."

I had a hunch what was coming next. "Carol don't tell us the story, again please," I said. Somehow, I knew she would.

Ignoring my plea Carol continued, "As I went to circle my Eugene for the third time, he took a step back, and landed on the train of my dress, causing me to trip and fall on my face. I was so embarrassed; I could have cried. Thank God the rabbi insisted we drink white wine during the ceremony. After the fall, as the rabbi said the wedding blessings, I had made a face at Eugene, who started laughing as he handed me the wine. I was so glad it wasn't red wine. He is such a klutz, but I do love him." We all laughed as she told the story, even though Mom and I had heard it many times.

Shira continued. "Then, we eat, drink and dance until everyone goes home. Oh yeah," Shira winced as she continued. "The men and women sit and dance separately, but you know that, right?" My eyes were tiring, and Shira was yawning so we said our goodbyes.

Around midnight, I drove Shira home. In the car, she confided, "I was initially nervous, but your mom and sister are quite sweet and made me feel welcome. I could tell your mom was nervous too. We are fortunate to have supportive loving families."

I turned toward Shira while keeping an eye on the road. "You are the first girl I ever brought home to meet my mom." That brought a huge smile to her face.

# The wedding

In New York, everyone knows someone. Everyone has a 'special guy' who will take care of you when it comes to jewelry, cameras and electronics. The peddlers boast that they can sell their merchandise for less because they get special deals from the factory or bought items that fell off the truck. I have represented many of these hawkers, who sell hot merchandise. Many have been charged for under-reporting their income or sales taxes or have been arrested for selling 'name brand' knockoff merchandise. I stay clear of my clients when I make my purchases. I never want to read my name in the newspapers, having acquired stolen items.

For our jewelry needs, my father had known and trusted Myron Toback. Our family shopped at his jewelry store on 47th Street for all our jewelry purchases. Shira and I walked into his shop and asked Myron for a plain, eighteen karat, yellow gold ring and a matching one karat diamond ring that could later be fashioned into one ring after the wedding. Shira bit her lower lip and kindly asked me if we could step outside for a moment to discuss the purchase.

Mr. Toback smiled. "Take your time; I'm not going anywhere."

We stepped away from the counter. Shyly, Shira looked down at my shoes and whispered, "Michael, I very much appreciate your generous gesture of the diamond ring. However, I will be just as happy with a gold wedding band. For me, that simple band will always have sentimental value. It's the symbol of our love that I will always wear and cherish. Please, if you don't mind, let's just buy the wedding band. I don't need the diamond."

We walked back to the counter and I thought to myself, any other girl would have wanted the biggest and the brightest diamond. Shira's gesture solidified that she was the one for me.

Myron had a display of white and yellow gold bands sitting on the counter. He knew exactly what we needed and what Shira wanted. "Give me two days and I will have the band you chose sized, polished and ready for pickup," he assured us.

On the following Shabbos, the aufruf ceremony went off without a hitch. The entire congregation delighted in showering us with candy and wishing us a sweet marriage. I was showered in the men's section, Shira in the woman's section, as the congregation serenaded us with song.

We returned to Shira's home for Shabbos lunch. For dessert, Emah pulled out a birthday cake from the kitchen. The family sang 'Happy Birthday' in English, Hebrew and Yiddish to Shira.

Today was September the sixth, Shira's eighteenth

birthday. If she hadn't been pregnant, I would have taken her back to my place that evening and opened a bottle of wine to toast the occasion. Instead, after lunch, we took a stroll down the block and held hands. "Shira, I bought you a combination engagement and birthday gift. Knowing that you would not tear the gift wrapping, I told them not to wrap it. I hope you like it."

Without seeing it she said, "Michael whatever it is, I will love it. Thank you." I handed her the small black velour box. Again, she thanked me and told me it was not necessary. She first read my handwritten note before she opened the box, peered at its contents and froze. She broke into tears once she saw what was inside.

I don't understand why women cry when they are thrilled and when they are sad. Shira was almost speechless. "This is beautiful." With reckless abandon, she ignored protocols and wrapped her arms around me and initiated a long, wet kiss.

She took off her Timex and I replaced it with an Omega Silver Lady's watch in white gold and diamonds. "Shira, I had been walking past Cartier on Fifty-Second and Fifth when I looked in the window and this watch called out to me. It said, "Buy me; she will love me." We both laughed. As we continued walking, she held my hand and put her head against my arm.

We returned to her home, and with her face glowing she ran into the kitchen to show her mother her gift. Shira remained there for ten minutes. I don't know what was said, but Emah opened the kitchen door, poked her head out, looked straight at me and smiled with her approval. I nodded and returned the smile.

A couple of days passed, and I attended Rosh Hashanah services with my Mom. I hadn't seen Shira since her birthday and missed her physical presence. We talked on the phone, but it wasn't the same. Jewish tradition dictates that the wedding couple remain apart and may not see each other for the week leading up to the ceremony. I physically missed touching and seeing her, but I guess that's the purpose of the tradition.

On the Tuesday before the wedding, Shira went to the mikvah to ritually bathe in preparation for our big day. I met with the Rav at his office at the yeshiva. The Rav traditionally met with couples prior to the ceremony to impart his wisdom. His daughter and I were no different.

He warmly greeted me at the door with a big hug and invited me to sit in the chair facing him. The Rav sat in an old wooden chair that slightly leaned to the left. His desk was heavily stained with watermarks and covered with a tower of papers and books at least three feet high. There were more books and texts scattered in every crevice of the room and floor. Behind him, there was a six-foot high window with a small, noisy, window air conditioner that barely cooled the room.

On the way to his office, I had passed a room where he consulted with dignitaries and paying clients. That room was plush, filled with ornate furniture and oriental rugs. I was told that some people pay five or six figures to have an audience with the Rav.

"Michael, I wanted to have this talk with you because I love my daughter and I understand that today couples need more than luck to have a lasting, good marriage. You have known my daughter for a relatively short amount of time."

Just then a man around my age interrupted us, carrying a stack of papers into Rav's office. "Rav, accept my apology. I need to disrupt your meeting. It will take just a moment of your time. These checks must be signed, bills must be paid today, and the mailman will be here anytime." Afterward, I learned that this was David Ben Aaron. It was his job to oversee the accounts payable duties at the shul and the yeshiva.

"Sorry, Michael, this will take just two seconds." I curiously watched as Rav blindly signed each check without examining them or the backup documentation. Then, he handed the pile of checks back to Mr. Aaron.

"Now, where were we? Yes, the two of you have grown up in different worlds. Both of you are going to need patience as you learn from the other. My daughter is younger and less experienced than you in the ways of the secular world. Shira will be entering a lifestyle which will be foreign to her. She will have no friends and no support system." He paused, and I surmised that he sought my response.

"Rav, I too have given thought to those very issues. These issues that you have addressed are of concern to me as well. I hope that each of us will make compromises for the sake of our marriage. We still have much to learn about each other. You are correct, Shira will know no one in Manhattan besides me. I will introduce her to my friends and their wives with the hopes they can become her friends too. Do you have any advice for us?"

"She will need you to be her best friend. You must allow her to occupy that role of your confidante with whom you trust your life. Share with Shira the inner thoughts you hold in your heart and keep no secret from her. The more you communicate the better your marriage will be. This is a time of transition for both of you, where you'll learn what works best for the two of you. You both need to be flexible, without compromising your moral values. For a marriage to succeed it takes unselfish hard work and a commitment to make it flourish."

We sat and talked for over an hour. When we parted, Rav placed his arm on mine. "Michael, I feel you have a righteous soul. God had a purpose bringing you and Shira together. It wasn't luck or by accident. In time, God will have a mission for you, and I will need you to be faithful and strong." I looked at him and contemplated if he truly was a mystic. Did he have a window into the future or was he merely speculating?

I left his office just as a limo pulled up and a man resembling Walter 'Clyde' Frazier of the Knicks appeared to be exiting the vehicle. The tall Afro-

American man proceeded into the yeshiva. I started my car engine and returned to thinking about the Rav's words and my new life with Shira. I wondered what kind of advice Clyde needed from Rav.

After our meeting, I looked forward to the day when Shira and I would be one. I couldn't wait for the time she would be in my bed every morning and night. The wedding was a mere couple of days away and I was truly excited.

On day of the wedding, I wore a black tux under the kittel, complemented with a red bow tie. Shira wore her sister Malka's satin wedding dress with a long train. In attendance were hundreds of people. I sat with her father at the tisch. The Rav offered me numerous toasts and poured me shots of eighteen-year-old scotch. I got lightheaded, but I don't think the alcohol fazed him. He leaned over, laughed and said, "We are drinking Scotch corresponding to Shira's age." I was too lightheaded to ask him why.

After more than thirty minutes of drinking, Shira's Emah and my mom entered the room with a glass plate wrapped in a napkin. Together, they smashed the plate on the table in front of me. Shira's father shouted, "Look! Just as the plate is shattered into pieces, so a broken relationship cannot be repaired. You must treat each other with respect and remember that your actions have consequences."

When the unveiling ceremony occurred and I saw my bride in her wedding dress for the first time, I was taken aback by her beauty. I was starstruck and grateful all at once for being blessed with this woman as my wife.

The ceremony was held outside under a baby blue sky with a slight breeze adding to a perfect day. Shira walked around me without incident. We shared the two cups of wine before I shattered the wine glass with the heel of my foot. The joke in Jewish circles is: "This is the last time the male will put his foot down during his marriage." Our guests yelled 'Mazel Tov!'"

I invited a number of my non-Jewish and Jewish friends. I was surprised how many responded that they would attend on such short notice. Sam Smith and George Andrews from the D.A.'s office said they wouldn't miss it. The three of us battle every day in court. Outside the courtroom, we have become trusted friends.

After the wedding ceremony, everyone walked back into the shul's social hall for dancing and drinking. Shira and I were escorted into the rabbi's study, where we were alone for seven minutes, after which we were permitted to join the festivities.

The Rav and his wife were carried around on chairs and hoisted to the ceiling by the strongest of the men. I danced with Rav, his sons, sons-in-law and countless other men until I was ready to drop. Shira danced with both our mothers, her sisters, my sister and two sisters-in-law while the band played, and scores of women danced the 'Hora'.

Finally, Shira and I were permitted to sit at the head table to cool off. The appetizers were served as the band played and guests danced. An hour later the main course arrived. In between the courses of food, there was more dancing and drinking. Mazel tov was shouted throughout the entire evening.

It was after midnight when the band stopped playing and the evening drew to a close. My shirt dripped with sweat, and I was physically exhausted. We took our gifts to the limousine and then, our driver drove us to our new home. Shira sat on my lap in the back of the limo. We kissed and talked about all that had transpired that day. We agreed it was a spectacular event and how fortunate we were.

Then, the initial mood killer. Shira said, "May I discuss something with you, but you must promise not to get angry?"

Warily, I said, "Yes."

She replied, "We received an awful amount of money tonight." With that she threw me for a loop. We just got married hours earlier and she had money concerns? Was this the same girl that I had known for the past six weeks?

Shira hesitated for a moment, bit her lip and then continued. "We have received financial gifts from friends and relative strangers. I was thinking. But, if you don't like my idea, please let me know. I would like us to donate a portion of the cash gifts, maybe ten percent, to a charitable bridal fund. It's a fund that makes dreams

97

come true for financially less well-off girls, those without a dowry, wedding dress or the means to fund a wedding ceremony. What do you think?"

I laughed with relief as I told her, "When you started this conversation, wanting to talk about money on our wedding day, you scared me. I love the idea. You are the best, most giving person in the world! This is why I married you. So, few brides would think of others on their special day. I don't know what to say, except that I love you and your kind heart." She blushed, not expecting the accolades.

We arrived home and I paid the limo driver. Just as the elevator closed, Shira pulled at my jacket lapel and with a devilish smile whispered in my ear. "I have something else to ask you."

"What?"

"Now that we're home, get me out of my dress and get me into our bed. I have found that pregnancy makes me sick in the mornings, but desirous of making love with you all the time. I have missed you this week, my bashert, my soulmate, my husband."

# Married life

Exhausted from hours of dancing and drinking on my wedding night, my body craved sleep. However, the emotions of being legally married and the chance to have sex with my wife was a powerful aphrodisiac. Our racing hormones were held in check for fifteen minutes, the time it took for me to carefully undo all the hooks securing Shira's dress.

It was a memorable evening. We made love with joy in our hearts, knowing in a few short months our family would be plus one. It was the first time we slept in a real bed together. When I close my eyes today, I can still fondly remember how radiant she looked that night.

Friday morning was our first official day as husband and wife. We had much to do before the start of Shabbos. For me, it was difficult getting out of bed after the previous night. It must have been tougher for Shira. Her body had to have ached, yet she somehow managed to get dressed without complaining.

She had a cup of coffee and a piece of toast smothered with sweet butter while I showered. I grabbed a Coke from the refrigerator as she grabbed two empty plastic food baskets from the closet, as we left the condo. In the lobby, I introduced Shira to Marvin, the morning doorman.

Once on the street I said, "Shira, the only way to learn the neighborhood is on foot. I hope you don't mind the walk."

"Don't worry, it's a beautiful day and I'm with you."

We walked to the kosher bakery, purchased challahs, a coffee cake, desserts and a couple of cold chocolate eclairs to eat as we continued our journey. The Friday traffic was bumper to bumper. Car horns blasted with drivers' frustration, the smog was intense and foot traffic was congested. Despite all of this, this was the city I loved!

We hiked three blocks to the butcher shop for two chickens, hamburger meat and a one-pound skirt steak. Then we returned to the condo to refrigerate the meat.

Once home Shira begged, "Michael, please let me take a nap," Shira pleaded.

"I feel badly for you, but we have to go to your parents. You can rest in the car. Did you forget that most of your clothes and belongings are still in Brooklyn?" She sadly nodded her head.

Once we arrived at her parents' place, Shira asked me, "Michael, do you have Shabbos candles?" I shrugged my shoulders. She replied, "Men."

She asked her mom for extra Shabbos candles. The suitcases and boxes were filled with not only her personal items but numerous gifts Emah thought we should have in our place. The bags and boxes we had to schlep back to the condo were heavy. We also stopped on the way to pick up fresh fruits and vegetables from a local stand before returning home.

As we rode up the elevator, Shira asked, "How do you get to shul in the morning? Don't tell me that you push the elevator button?"

I had to embarrassingly laugh. "Yes, Shira, I use the elevator. But I keep Shabbos. I don't work, travel or use the telephone. However, I do the following: I press the buttons on the elevator. I turn the oven and stove on and off. And I leave the television on in the guest room, so I can watch the Yankee games." She closed her eyes and shook her head, but a small smile formed on her lips.

As we walked into the condo, she stated the obvious. "Michael, we have much to learn about each other. You're lucky I love you with all my heart. We have plenty of time before Shabbos. I'm going to take a nap." In no time, her body collapsed into bed where she yawned and said, "Wake me no later than 5:00 p.m. so I can prepare dinner." I offered to cook, but she was insistent.

Refreshed from her nap, Shira dressed for Shabbos in her finest attire and cooked a meal fit for a king. I helped her with the cleanup and then we relaxed in the living room. She sat next to me with my arm around her shoulders. "What's your normal routine on Shabbos day?"

"Normally, I walk over to the traditional shul and arrive by 8:45 a.m., a few minutes before the beginning of prayers. After services, there is a sparse, light kiddush which leaves me hungry, so I return home and grab a bite to eat. Later in the afternoon, I go over to the park to play some basketball with my friends, go for a run or watch a game, depending upon the day."

"What is a traditional shul?"

"It is an orthodox service with one exception; men and women sit together."

Surprised, Shira simply said, "Oh."

"If you want, Shira, we can go to the orthodox shul instead."

She considered all options before she committed herself. "Why do you prefer one over the other?"

"I grew up and attended public school. The guys at the orthodox minyan all went to yeshiva or cheder together and it's very cliquey and not welcoming to strangers. I have made friends at the traditional shul and socialize with them during the week. They're normal guys like me."

"Michael, I have never sat with men in a service. I'm not sure how comfortable it will be. However, I will join you at the traditional shul tomorrow morning. At least I won't be sitting with a stranger." I knew she would feel awkward in a mixed seating forum. Her concession was appreciated. It meant a lot to me.

After dinner, we retreated to the bedroom. Shira asked, "Would you mind rubbing my lower back? It's been aching all day. I made light of it when my sisters complained that their entire bodies ached. Until now, I never knew how uncomfortable pregnancy could be." Our first Friday night together was romantic. The candles flickered for hours after we retired to our bed.

The next morning, Shira and I had a light breakfast and walked to the elevator. Shira pretended not to see me press the elevator buttons. She was dressed like a prim and proper religious wife, sporting a shul hat.

Upon entering the shul, friends came up to us and offered their congratulations. At kiddush, I formally introduced Shira to them, and she appeared comfortable conversing with the wives.

During the services, I noticed Shira prayed with conviction. Shira seemed to feel the words, as if they came from her soul and went directly to God's ears. When the Torah portion was read, I pointed something out in the reading and asked her a question. She explained the meaning of the passage to me. However, she refused to allow me to hold her hand during the rabbi's sermon. She admonished me with a playful slap on my hand.

Upon returning home, we sat down for lunch. During the meal I asked, "So tell me, how was shul for you today?"

"It was quieter than my Aba's shul. I concentrated on my prayers and enjoyed the interaction of studying the Torah portion with you. I appreciated that your friends came over to introduce themselves. The wives seemed kind and friendly. Let's go back next Shabbos and see how it goes."

"No, dear, tomorrow night is Yom Kippur. We will be back at shul sooner than next week. By the way, you met Joel briefly today. He's about my height, dark hair and black glasses. Joel and his wife have invited us to their apartment to break the fast with their family. We invited them to the wedding, but they couldn't attend."

"On Monday, Yom Kippur day, I have worked it out with Marvin, the doorman, that when you return home to rest, drink or eat, he will push the elevator button for you without you asking."

Shira moved her head from side to side and said, "I was thinking that I would like to play it by ear on Monday if I need to have a drink."

I felt a need to express my feelings. "Shira, you are pregnant. According to Jewish law as you so well know, you are permitted to eat and drink, if not for you, for the health of our child. So, please don't be a hero."

In a sarcastic tone she answered, "Yes, Michael."

I prayed with conviction as I normally do every Yom Kippur. On this day, I believe that God decides who will live and who will die during the coming year. I implored God for forgiveness. I begged God for a good and healthy year. I prayed for Shira and the health of our child. I looked over at my wife and asked her how she was doing. She appeared worn out. I made sure that she took a break to rest around 2 p.m., if for nothing else, to put her feet up.

My favorite part of the Yom Kippur service is the concluding Neilah service. After fourteen hours in shul and twenty-five hours of fasting, the Neilah service begins. Men and women of all ages, including the elderly, stand for the next hour. They sing praises to God at the top of their lungs even as parched throats crave water and bellies rumble for food. Shira and I left after services concluded, hungry but with uplifted spirits.

As the sun set and the holiday ended, we walked over to Joel's and joined some twenty-five guests for food and drinks. Joel's food tables were laden with bagels, cream cheese, lox, cheese blintzes and pastries. I smiled as Joel and his wife walked over to greet us. Joel's wife was a slender woman with dark hair and a small frame.

"Thank you for joining us. My name is Sara. I'm Joel's wife. Congratulations on your marriage. You married a great guy." She started to walk away but stopped, slowly turned around and said, "Up close, you look awfully familiar. Did you ever live in Brooklyn?"

"Yes, how did you guess? My maiden name, was Lefkovitz."

Sara laughed. "I went to school with your sister, Malka. Yes, I now see the resemblance. Join me as I check on my son. I'm sure he's not sleeping with all this commotion. We have so much to talk about." They entered the nursery and found him standing in the crib in need of a diaper change.

Shira asked Sara, "Tell me, how did you make the transition from Brooklyn to Manhattan?"

105

"Shira, it's a long story. Tomorrow, if you have time, let's meet in the morning for coffee." Shira nodded yes. "How about coming over at 9 a.m.? I am dying to talk to someone from the old neighborhood and no one from here would know what I was talking about." With the diaper changed and baby resting in his bed, the two women walked out of the nursery toward the commotion filled living room.

"Perfect, I'll see you tomorrow," said Shira. "By the way, what's your son's name?"

"Adam. Forgive me, I'll see you tomorrow. Right now, I need to play hostess. Go, please eat." Sara walked into the kitchen as Shira joined me in the living room.

Years later, Shira confided in me that she had needed to talk with someone who would understand the cultural shock she was experiencing. The traditional shul wasn't the rigid orthodox shul she had known all her life. I would later learn that the Shabbos use of the elevator and the stove really bothered Shira, but she didn't tell me at the time because our relationship was too new.

The following morning, Shira arrived promptly at Sara's place carrying fresh, hot pastries from the bakery. Sara was feeding Adam. In the space of an hour, they became fast friends. They had so much in common it was almost eerie.

As I look back, I realize it was Sara who was most responsible for Shira's transition from Brooklyn to the big city. For the first time in her life, Shira began to wear slacks, something frowned upon where she grew up. She told me that stretch pants had more support as her belly blossomed, but I knew she liked the comfort of slacks.

That night, when I returned from the office, Shira told me about her morning with Sara. Shira told Sara how we met, leaving out the drugs and sex. "Michael, the rest of the time, it was just girls' talk. I really like her. Her son, Adam, is the cutest little guy."

What she didn't tell me was that Sara offered her ideas so that Shabbos would feel more comfortable in a Manhattan high-rise. First, Sara told Shira, "Take charge. You want more company for Shabbos, then invite them over to your place or ask to be invited out to theirs. Men are lazy. Nothing gets done unless a woman initiates it. I guarantee if you set the ground rules, Michael may gripe at first, then he will do what you tell him. It worked with Joel. Oh, don't ever tell Michael that I said that, okay?" Shira laughed and agreed.

"How did you two meet and decide to live here in Manhattan?"

"We met at the City College. I was living at home at the time. My parents didn't want me to attend college and were upset that I chose to delay finding a spouse until I graduated. Joel was in one of my classes. We secretly dated for three months before he met my parents. He wasn't religious and never attended services before he met me. I thought after talking to my Dad he would leave me for another, and my parents would lock me in my bedroom."

Intrigued Shira asked, "What happened next?"

"The next week, he proposed to me on the condition that we would not live in Brooklyn. I agreed on the condition he become more religious, observe Shabbos and attend shul." She took a sip of coffee. "He learned to enjoy it and we have a wonderful marriage. Though he freaks out when we spend a holiday in Brooklyn." They both laughed and understood.

Shira listened to Sara's advice and gradually took control of our home and ownership of Shabbos. Almost every Friday night we had guests over or we walked over to a friend's place for dinner. On Saturdays, we developed a routine of taking afternoon naps and strolling in the park when weather permitted. Twice a month, she initiated a study group at our home where a yeshiva student instructed us and two other couples in Jewish law: Mishnah and Talmud.

We had created our own community of friends, some from the shul, others from around the neighborhood. As for the elevator, Shira frequently said that she would have taken the stairs had it not been for the baby she was carrying. "Michael, I hate taking the elevator on Shabbos. I apologize to God every time you press the button." Then, I would laugh.

# I had a lot to learn

For the first couple of months of our marriage, I found myself working like there was no tomorrow. As I look back now, I see that I was becoming my workaholic father, rather than the sensitive husband Shira needed. My office was extremely busy. I was worried about money with a child on the way, even though I was financially well off with plenty of new cases being opened every week.

We represented a couple of police officers who were caught up in the Knapp Commission. This scandal became known publicly in April 1970 and involved police corruption driven by the revelations of patrolman Frank Serpico and Sergeant David Durk. The word on the street was that Mayor John V. Lindsay was on a mission to get rid of bad cops well before the commission was formed. My firm represented numerous city employees who worried about the consequences of bribes they had received over the years.

Late one afternoon, Pat walked into my office. "Mikey, you are working day, nights and Sundays. Do you want to destroy your marriage? Shira needs you at home more than you need to be here. Hire another associate before it's too late."

"Pat, Shira is studying for her classes, spending time with her friends and we have tons of cases that need to be worked on."

"Mikey, when was the last time you took your wife out on the town, out for dinner and a movie?"

I thought about it for a couple of seconds and had to admit, she was right. I called Shira as Pat left my office and despite Shira's protests, I told her I was taking her out for dinner. I thanked Pat as I left the office and told her I appreciated her speaking up and imparting her words of wisdom to me.

Shira confessed that she had a craving for chopped liver with onions and a juicy, hot pastrami sandwich on rye. I was thinking more like steaks at a white tablecloth restaurant. Instead, we ate at Abe Lebewohl's tiny, ten-seat deli at Second Avenue and East Tenth Street. I enjoyed watching Shira lick her fingers between courses and telling her that the mustard was smudged on the side of her cheek.

Abe made each sandwich with half a pound of meat. Thankfully, Shira took half of the sandwich home. However, the onion rings were consumed in a flash. I was able to grab a couple for myself without my fingers getting slapped.

Between mouthfuls, I apologized to Shira for my insensitivity. Together, we made a pact to have date night every Sunday and Wednesday nights. "What if I get tickets for a Broadway musical next week?" I said.

Shira responded, "I have never seen a Broadway musical. I heard they are phenomenal. Is that true?" Her words silenced me as once again it hit me how profoundly different our worldly experiences were.

"I will get us tickets and you will decide."

On the way home, Shira began to feel the effects of the food. She made me promise to never let her eat so much at one time again, as she continued to lick mustard from the side of her mouth. At home, I gave Shira two Alka-Seltzer tablets and a glass of water to relieve her indigestion. As the commercial says, 'Oh, what a relief it is.'

The following week, we attended the Broadway musical '1776'. She sat there like a child. The glow on her face and laughter from her belly were my rewards. At one time she told me that she laughed so hard she almost peed. Then, I remembered she was only eighteen. During the entire ride home, Shira talked about the play and how much she enjoyed it. The second play we saw was 'Canterbury Tales'. It was equally as good. In no time, Shira became hooked on Broadway theater.

Thanks to my wife, my condo became our 'home'. Thanks to Pat and Sara, we learned what it meant to be a married couple.

Joel, Sara and Adam came over for dinner at least once a month or we went to their place. They became our best friends. Most weekends, we went to a movie theater or played Scrabble and card games at one of our homes.

Joel and I were at a Knicks' game and I asked how they met. "I met Sara in school; I didn't know what she meant when she said she was religious. I corrupted her by getting her to kiss me and in doing so, I fell in love with her. Originally, she wanted to live in Brooklyn, but after meeting the clan, I told her that would be a deal breaker. So, we compromised. She is the best thing that ever happened to me. I'm so lucky. Her parents still wish she married a religious yeshiva student." We both had a good laugh afterwards.

We were three months away from Shira's due date. I came home one evening and approached Shira with the idea of attending a birthing class as a couple.

"Shira, I heard from someone at the courthouse about a program called the 'Lamaze Method'. It meets twice a week in the evenings at Mount Sinai hospital. The program will teach us how to prepare for the baby's delivery in the hospital. It's a couples' thing. You know more than I do about babies, but I thought it would be fun." I showed her the brochure and she began leafing through the pages.

"Michael, it says you would be in the birthing room with me. Are you okay with that?"

"Shira, I want to be there for you and right now, I don't know what to do or not to do."

"So, let's do it. Maybe it will be fun. I've heard of husbands fainting at the sight of blood. I hope you can handle it." Then she giggled.

"Funny. Very funny."

Beginning in February, we braved the cold, snowy weather, and traveled to the hospital carrying a pillow and bag of goodies. It was a blast. The instructors taught expectant moms how to breathe when in labor to control the pain and weather the contractions. The guys acted as coaches. As coaches, we encouraged our spouses to use proper breathing techniques and reminded them we loved them.

The guys fed Popsicles or lollipops to their wives when they were thirsty as we role played labor. We were told that once the doctor administered anesthetics in the hospital, the women would not be permitted to drink. The Popsicles and lollipops were to prevent the expectant moms' getting dry mouth. We were also taught the essential items to pack for the hospital. We packed our bag well in advance of the due date just in case.

We made friends with three couples in the class and would hang out with them. After class, if the expectant Moms weren't too tired, we went for tea and talked about our wives' discomfort. Months after the birth of our respective children, the new moms set up play dates, got together for adult conversations and shared parenting tips as the kids lay on their blankets between feedings.

At the end of the Lamaze program, it was announced that prior to our graduating class, husbands were permitted in the birthing rooms only until the actual birth began and then they were required to leave. By completing the Lamaze course, the hospital would now permit husbands to stay in the room with our wives during the entire labor and delivery process.

Initially, I was apprehensive, but as I thought through the concept, I welcomed the idea of being supportive when she needed me most. I feared the unknown prospect of fainting at the first sign of blood and knowing that Shira would never let me forget that she told me so.

We came close to having a verbal disagreement two weeks before Shira's due date. She refused a baby shower. She feared the 'Evil Eye' would cause something bad to happen to the baby if we had baby furniture and clothes delivered to our home before the birth. I was worried. It was my nature to have everything organized and planned ahead of time.

Feeling the stress, I started to shout at Shira. I caught myself and apologized. "I'm sorry for raising my voice. But we have no baby clothes, no furniture, and you keep telling me not to worry. I can't stop worrying. It's in my DNA."

Somehow, Shira kept her cool and whispered that everything was handled. "Sara will bring over a bassinet, changing table and crib after the birth. My sisters are gathering baby clothes for us. Don't worry. Please call the guys and go out and play basketball or go for a run. You need it. Besides, you are driving me crazy!"

On May fifteenth, 1970, our son was born. I must confess, while Shira was in labor, suffering in pain, I kept one eye on her and the other on the telecast of the Knicks game in her room. Emah came to see her grandson and the first thing she did was tie a red string around his tiny wrist. Out of ignorance, I asked Shira once Emah left, "What's up with the red string? Should I take it off?"

With a shocked face, Shira emphatically said, "No! Don't touch that string! It's to ward off evil spirits."

"C'mon, you don't really believe in this nonsense, do you?"

"Of course not, but just in case, don't remove the red thread!" I snickered.

"Michael, tradition tells us that a male child doesn't receive his soul until his bris. By not naming him, we are not allowing the angel of death the opportunity to identify our child. We need to protect him from Satan before the bris. So, we mustn't name him, or tell people the name that we have chosen until after the bris. Okay?"

I had to laugh. Never in my wildest dreams would I have suspected that my wife had a superstitious nature. "Shira, my mom is on the way. She will want to know his name. You will need to explain it to her." In the back of my mind, I was toying with the idea of giving our son the middle name, 'Van', but I knew that would not go over well.

My mom walked in. "So, what is his name? Or are

you waiting to name him at the bris?" Shira smiled. My mom looked at me. "Son don't look so shocked. Your grandfather wouldn't let us name you before your bris either."

The bris was at Rav's Brooklyn home. People were packed in every room and down the narrow stairwell. There was no space to accommodate another soul in the apartment. My mom and Carol's family entered the apartment by way of the backstairs to bypass the onlookers.

The mohel who performed the bris had to be seventy years old and weighed at least two hundred and seventy-five pounds. He was a Hasidic rabbi with a bushy, gray beard who had circumcised at least ten thousand eight-day old males.

It was extremely warm in the apartment, due to the cramped conditions and the size of the crowd. I had the job of wiping the sweat from the mohel's forehead as he performed the ceremony. Rav dipped a white cloth into the wine and fed it to our son. I continued to hope and pray that the mohel's sweaty hands would remain steady during the entire procedure. Shira couldn't bear to watch, and then breathed a huge sigh of relief once the procedure was completed.

We were immensely proud to present our son to the world, Benjamin (Ben) who was named after my father the Mohel explained. After the ceremony, everyone joined in and yelled 'Mazel tov'!

There was plenty of food for those lucky enough to

reach the table. The apartment was stifling. I couldn't wait to drive Shira and Ben home. It was a tough day for all of us.

Two days after the bris, the Knicks completed their championship run. Horns, whistles and fireworks lit up the evening sky that night. Shira thought New York was celebrating our good fortune.

That first year, was one of transition as we learned from one another and crafted a way of life acceptable for both of us. We created our community of friends and settled on a religious observance we could agree to. I learned quickly that life was less complicated when I agreed with my wife's wishes. Important decisions we made jointly.

After the pregnancy, Shira resumed her studies. I don't know where she found the energy to accomplish all she did. As I had hoped, our moms agreed to take turns babysitting on the days Shira attended classes and willingly came over to our place more often if we needed assistance.

My law practice and the size of my law firm grew which created additional demands for my time. I began representing high-profile, big paying criminal cases and found my name mentioned in the newspapers. The workload caused me to work some evenings, but I never miss a date night.

We were fortunate to find a thirteen-year-old girl named Debbie who lived on our floor and loved to babysit for Ben. Debbie made it possible for us to get out of the house and relax for a couple of hours during the week.

During the Jewish holiday of freedom, Chanukah, twenty-thousand Jews in New York held a protest rally in Madison Square Garden. The protesters demanded the United States apply economic pressure against the Soviet Union until it permitted Jews the right to secure exit visas without punishment. Much of the nation's activism for Soviet Jewry was centered here in New York. This particular protest, I attended the rally with Rav at his suggestion.

In Washington D.C., there were ongoing negotiations with the Soviet Union. In May 1972, the Soviets signed the Strategic Arms Limitation Talks (SALT) One Treaty with the United States that led to the freezing of strategic ballistic missiles. During the negotiations, the Soviets were concerned that American Jews were beginning to create a firestorm with members of the U.S. Congress to press for Jewish emigration.

There was a secret agreement attached to the SALT One negotiations, where the Nixon administration agreed they would perform the necessary actions to discourage U.S. Jews from influencing the U.S. government policies that would punish the Soviet Union for human rights' abuses.

The freedom movement in the U.S. demanded the release of some of the brightest and best Soviet Jewish scientists. Activists demanded that Soviet Jewish citizens be permitted to relocate in Israel or the U.S. The pressure appeared to be working as both Washington and Moscow cowered.

Richard Nixon met with Leonid Brezhnev, General Secretary of the governing Communist Party of the Soviet Union to establish détente. Right before their meeting, the Soviets levied an emigration tax and education tax on those who sought to emigrate from the Soviet Union.

Henry Kissinger and President Nixon were reluctant to broach the subject of human rights' abuses during the negotiations. Their reluctance emboldened the Soviets and caused them to institute harsher conditions on their Jewish citizens. Senators and congressmen like Senator Henry Jackson stood up to the White House and spearheaded efforts to punish the Soviets unless they changed their abusive internal policies.

Shira read a biography written by a journalist for the Israeli newspaper, 'Haaretz'. She shared the book with me. It was called 'Jews of Silence', written by Elie Wiesel. It gave me insight into the living conditions of the Jews in the Soviet Union. Shira also turned me on to another book that Wiesel authored, 'Night'. Each of his books were emotionally moving and caused me to want to broaden my Jewish education. The plight of Soviet Jews became a concern of mine and I donated monies to support them.

On Saturday afternoons, when I couldn't play basketball, Shira had an opportunity to take a nap, so she could replenish the spirit in her body after her long week of being a mom, student and wife. More importantly, it gave me time with Ben, one-on-one. Without wishing away time, I imagined Ben and I going to the park to play catch.

Years melted away before I knew it. We were in our third year of marriage. The year was 1972. Ben was teaching us about the 'terrible twos'. His favorite word was 'no'. One Shabbos his loving mother made him a PB& J sandwich when he refused to eat dinner. She cut off the crust and gave him a sippy cup of milk.

The next year was our roughest. The year began with a bad omen when major league baseball went on strike for twelve days in April. Thank God, the strike ended early. Up until then, my marriage was a storybook, fairy tale romance. Little did I suspect that forces beyond our control would challenge us in ways that defied comprehension. Misery would soon arrive at our doorstep. Rav's prediction came true.

# The phone call

The black rotary phone in our bedroom rang. It was 5 a.m. Shira grabbed it. With one eye closed and the other half open she answered it with her mind still groggy, "Who's this?"

In a hushed tone, so as not to be overheard, a male voice said, "Shira, its George Andrews. It's urgent. Wake Mike up." George had attended our wedding and I played basketball with him at the park during the summer. She remembered that he worked at the district attorney's office.

Shira shook me with her free elbow and handed me the phone. My head remained on the pillow and my eyes remained shut. Before I could say, "What's up?" George interrupted me.

"Get to your father-in-law's place, now! He's going to be arrested. The newspaper and television camera crews are on the way. I gotta go before someone hears me talking to you. You owe me."

Shira scornfully mumbled, "Michael, please tell your friends not to call until after eight. Ben and I need our sleep."

"Shira, this was an important call! Get up and call Emah right now! Don't ask any questions. Tell your parents to get dressed this minute. I am leaving for their place as soon as I get dressed. Don't tell them anything, and do not mention George's name. Assume their phones are being tapped. No questions. Call them this very second."

Frantically, I brushed my teeth, threw on a suit and shoes skipping my morning shower. Shira was a nervous wreck, yet all I could tell her was that her father was being arrested. Her face turned white, and her mouth was agape as her eyes were consumed with fear.

Arriving at Rav's home, I found the media vultures had blocked off the street with their camera-mounted trucks. I had to park a couple of blocks away. As I walked to their building, I smiled and waved to the cops, reporters and the district attorney, all of whom were acquaintances of mine. I always told my staff it's better to have them as friends than enemies.

I went upstairs and confronted Rav. "We have very little time. The police are on the way to arrest you. Do not say a word! Let me do all the talking. Emah, open the front door. Otherwise, they may break it down."

In a smug, indignant tone, Rav said, "I did nothing wrong! You must be mistaken! They don't arrest innocent people in America."

"Look out your window! Tell me if crews from half the television stations in New York aren't downstairs." As he peered out the window, I continued. "The police will read you your rights. They will cuff you and drag you down the street in front of the cameras to embarrass you in the hope you will talk or say something in anger that can be used against you at your trial. Say nothing! Do you understand me?" I raised my voice to express the seriousness of the situation.

I found myself laying down the law to Rav in a manner that I would speak to any other criminal client with the hope my words would sink in. I was direct and to the point. I had switched from the respectful son-in-law to the hard-as-nails criminal attorney focused on serving my client. Rav was initially taken back by the manner he was being spoken to but started to realize the gravity of the situation.

Emah was crying and wasn't her rational self. Calming words of reassurance from her husband fell on deaf ears as fear overwhelmed her. I walked over and opened the front door that Emah failed to open, just as the cops picked up a black metal battering ram.

One of the disappointed cops, standing there in his short-sleeved shirt with the '63rd Precinct' insignia on his lapel, said in a noticeable Irish brogue, "Ah, Mikey, what ya doing? I love this part of my job."

"Sorry, Flynn. They're family. Next time, I'll double lock the door, just for you." Flynn smiled as Joe Marcus from the district attorney's office entered the apartment. Flynn placed the handcuffs on the Rav's wrists as ordered.

I pleaded, "Joe, how long have we known each other? Five years? I've always been straight with you, right? Mr. Lefkovitz is my father-in-law. He's over sixty years old. Can I bring him into the station and bypass the cameras? Can we not cuff him? He's a rabbi for God's sake."

"Mikey, I've got my orders. They want the 'perp-walk' in cuffs and in front of the cameras. This is an election year. The district attorney needs publicity to help him in his re-election bid." Then Joe Marcus handed me the papers and said, "Here's your copy of the search and arrest warrants. The warrants cover the home, the temple and the yeshiva. Any problems with the warrants, take it up with the man downtown."

Joe walked over to the Rav and read him his Miranda rights. Then Joe asked the Rav if he understood his rights. The Rav simply said, "Yes." I could tell that the humiliation of shame of being arrested had taken hold.

The 'perp-walk' is a frequent practice in American law enforcement. An individual is arrested, cuffed and publicly humiliated by being paraded in front of the television and news cameras. New York's district attorney and the U.S. assistant attorneys have a bad reputation for demeaning and degrading infamous individuals in this manner.

Flynn was apologetic. "Mikey," he said, pointing to the Rav, "he couldn't put his arms behind his back without discomfort and his wrists were quite large, so I cuffed in the front and left them loose."

"Flynn, there is a place in heaven for you. I owe you big time."

"Mikey, let heaven know, I'm not ready to die anytime soon." We both laughed.

Joe took the Rav's arm and walked him down the two flights of stairs, pausing in front of the apartment building to show off the prize, so the press and the cameras had their close-up shots. Reporters shouted out their questions as the Rav stood there in earshot of them with his cuffed hands raised, covering his face.

Then, Joe pushed the Rav into the back seat of the squad car, a blue 1971 Plymouth Fury. Once inside the car, reporters continued shouting their questions through the partially opened windows. One aggressive photographer butted the lens of the camera through the open window for a close-up shot. The Rav faced forward, pretending that he was alone and unfazed. In his heart he wanted to curse them all.

The reporters shoved their microphones into the car and in the Rav's face. They asked a barrage of stupid questions meant to embarrass him. "Did God tell you to steal and for what purpose?"

"How much did you steal?"

"Is it true you took millions from the charity?" With each question the anger in his belly swelled. Finally, the squad car pulled away.

I wasn't allowed in the police car. My parting advice reiterated to the Rav, "Don't say anything. No matter what, remain silent. They will intentionally misconstrue your words later against you, so say nothing."

Rav later confessed that the cops tried to goad him into confessing as they made their way to the station. "So, you're a religious guy, huh?" The Rav initially remained silent.

"You fucking Jews like money, don't yah? You guys own the banks and the jewelry stores, huh? How much did you steal? What did you do with the money? Buy your wife a fur coat?"

Then the driver retorted, "Didn't you see the ugly wife, he probably spent the money on the whores on Forty-Second Street."

Rav shamefully admitted, "Michael, I was unable to hold my tongue any longer. I questioned, in Yiddish, whether the cop's mother mated with a sewer rat. I regretted saying it. As soon as the words came out of my mouth, I realized that these individuals caused me to lose my temper. In doing so, I temporarily lost trust that God would save me from my enemies. I will never let it happen again. I have prayed for his forgiveness ever since."

The car pulled up to the 63rd Precinct police station in Brooklyn, located on Brooklyn Avenue. I was waiting for Rav in the parking lot when the squad car arrived. I helped him out of the vehicle. Then, we walked up the steps into the crowded precinct, and walked further up more creaking stairs inside the station to reach the criminal processing area. That was where the Rav's cuffs were removed. He was fingerprinted and his mug shot taken. The Jewish sergeant handed the Rav a wet paper towel to clean the ink from his fingers.

Escorted by a police officer, we went up more flights of stairs to the office that housed the precinct's detectives. Rav's hand grasped the metal railing for stability and support. He assured me he was nothing more than winded from all the stairs. I was hoping that the ordeal wasn't triggering a heart attack.

The walls had the smell of fresh paint. There were patches of plaster missing from the ceiling. The oak wood floors had been recently painted and were still drying after being mopped that morning. Window air conditioning units were operating on the west side of the building, yet the room was quite warm and musty.

The detective's room had a pungent odor that seemed to combine the smells of liquor, body odor, vomit and cigarettes. Each detective sat at his desk smoking, casting the ashes and butts to the ground. On the wall opposite the windows was the temporary criminal holding cell. There was a bench, accommodating at most six prisoners however, there were fifteen people currently standing or sitting in the cell.

The detective assigned to our case was a gray-haired Caucasian with a few extra pounds around his waist. The name on the badge read 'Shaun O'Keefe'. He spoke with a lit Camel cigarette dangling from his lips and had alcohol on his breath. He wore a stained, wrinkled shirt and loosely knotted tie around his neck. Around his chest he packed a sub-nose thirty-eight revolver on his left side. His words were a little slurred as every other word was, "Uh" or "Yah know." He was old-school.

"What's your name?" asked Shaun.

I answered on the Rav's behalf. "Rabbi Moshe Lefkovitz."

"Who are you? Is this guy a deaf mute?"

"I am his attorney; my name is Michael Goldman. I will answer all of your questions."

As I replied to the detective's questions, Shaun recorded my answers on a Royal electric typewriter as his two index fingers pounded on the keys. They moved as fast as he could find the keys. If I didn't know the answer, Rav would tell me, and I'd then relayed the answer to Shaun.

Shaun motioned to me with his head. "Mikey, can I call you Mikey?" I nodded that it was okay. "Join me in the other room." He put Rav in a communal holding cell. Then, Shaun and I walked to a conference room lined with mirrored, one-way glass. This room was bugged with microphones. The D.A. and others typically watched interrogations from behind the glass without the bad guy's knowledge.

"Mike, you seem like a nice guy. We got him. We have the bank records; the signed checks and we have witnesses. If he cooperates and confesses, I'll have a talk with the district attorney and ask him to be lenient. Right now, the indictment will read money laundering, bribing public officials and embezzlement of funds.

That could be a life sentence for a guy his age."

In a professional tone, I responded, "Detective, give me an opportunity to talk to my client and we will consider your offer."

I had no intention of agreeing to anything. I had no idea the substance of the charges. I needed time to learn from my client what the hell was going on. How could the rabbi be involved in such criminal activities? He was such a pious ethical individual from everything that I observed over the years. I was shocked by the charges and couldn't believe what I was hearing from Shaun as he read the arrest warrant.

The Rav was sharing a cell with an assortment of drunks, pimps and a couple of suspected thieves. His response was to face east, with his body moving back and forth, with his hands occasionally raised in the air as he recited his morning prayers with conviction. He was begging God to save him. Unfortunately, he didn't have his tallis or his tefillin to wear as he prayed. I asked Shaun not to disturb the rabbi until he finished.

With his prayers concluded, Shaun attempted to move Rav and me to an interrogation room to confer in private. "Detective, I prefer a room without one-way windows and microphones," I told him. The detective smiled and chuckled. Shaun was sly one and obviously couldn't be trusted.

Once situated in another room, I leaned over to my father-in-law and pleaded. "The only way I can help you is if you tell me the entire truth." I raised my hands,

"What's going on here?"

He made a gesture, moving his hands to his side with his palms facing the heavens. "Michael, I'm not sure I didn't perform any illegal acts. This must be a mistake."

Agitated, I stared directly into his eyes and frankly said, "Rav, tell me what you think wasn't a crime."

"Michael, I raise a lot of money from wealthy people. I consult and offer advice. These individuals renumerate me when I provide them answers to questions that plague them."

"Okay, where does the money go?"

"Some money is used to fund the shul and the yeshiva's operations. Some monies are distributed to the poor. They use the funds to pay their rent, medical bills, the cost of a daughter's wedding, or feed their family."

My voice grew harsh. "So, you are telling me that they arrested you for feeding the poor? And all these monies were used for no other clandestine purpose?"

"Well…" After a pregnant pause and a sigh, he continued. "We assist in the smuggling of refuseniks out of Russia and into the United States. We do so with a visa that we obtain for them through our Congressman."

"What are refuseniks and how do you smuggle them out of Russia?"

"Refuseniks are Soviet Jews who have applied for visas and been denied permission to leave Russia." I never knew there was a name for those denied Soviet exit visas. The Rav continued. "These brave souls pay a harsh penalty for applying for a Russian exit visa. The refuseniks lose or get demoted from their jobs or expelled from the universities where they are enrolled. Some are beaten up, sentenced to prison, sent to Siberia and their families are punished. Without work, they can't buy food or pay rent. The Russian thugs beat them bloody if they continue to defy the Soviet government."

"So, how involved are you in the protest movement and what exactly do you do? Why didn't you tell me about your involvement before now? I've attended rallies to with you and you never said anything? Why?"

Just then, there was a knock at the door. I yelled, "Detective, please give me a few more minutes to confer with my client."

"Sorry Mikey. I can't. The feds are here, and they are taking over the case." I stepped out of the room and looked over toward the detective's desk. There stood two fit, Caucasian males with neatly trimmed hair, identical stylish gray suits and polished shoes.

I walked my father-in-law over to what I assumed were two federal agents. One extended his hand. "I am Special Agent Johns, and this is my partner, Special Agent Murphy. We are Special Agents with the FBI. We're here to interrogate Rabbi Moshe Lefkovitz and bring him in for additional questioning."

"What are the charges?" I knew this was getting more serious as the minutes ticked by, yet I was still clueless as to what the Rav actually did. Everyone knew more than I did, which is a terrible position for an attorney to be in.

"I assume you are his attorney?" I nodded my head. Murphy looked at the rabbi and said, "Gather up your belongings. We are going to our offices at the federal building."

"Special Agent Johns, my client is an overweight Jewish rabbi. Is it possible we could walk to your vehicle without the cuffs?"

Johns strangely changed his tune and I stood there momentarily baffled. "Counselor, we are here to invite Rabbi Lefkovitz to sit down with us for a formal interview. It will be your client's opportunity to discuss the financial operations of his businesses and his involvement in those endeavors before charges are pressed. He could clear up all possible questions we have regarding his personal involvement in criminal activities."

"Special Agent Johns, may I have the day to meet with my client? I promise to agree to an interview tomorrow morning, subject to us receiving a proffer agreement. I promise you; it will be a more productive meeting if I am prepared."

"Counselor, I assume you know the Emanuel Celler Federal Building, it is in the Civic Center of Brooklyn?"

"Yes, I am familiar with it."

"I will see you at 10 a.m. tomorrow morning. Ask for me or special Agent Murphy at the downstairs security desk. We will meet you and escort you upstairs to our offices."

After Rav signed some paperwork and retrieved his confiscated personal belongings, we walked out of the Brooklyn police station. I could tell that he was not the same man who woke up that morning. He had aged considerably in the span of a few hours. Nothing is more humbling than standing in a jail cell a few feet from a drunk who is throwing up his guts.

We walked over to my car in the parking lot. I opened the passenger door. The Rav sat down in the front seat. Emotionless, his eyes stared forward, as if he was a zombie. I couldn't but notice that his wrinkled hands shook from the ordeal. I drove him to my home, so I could interview him thoroughly knowing we'd be alone and without outside interruptions.

Earlier that morning, Shira had wanted to join me on the ride to Brooklyn, but I convinced her that she'd be in the way. I knew she had a mid-term test and I encouraged her to attend her class. Ben was at my mom's place, so our home was quiet.

I called my office. "Pat, tell me, what's going on?"

"Your father-in-law's arrest was plastered all over the morning news. Where are you?"

"I'm with him at my place. Can you ask the associates to handle all my court matters today? It appears that I will be with my father-in-law for the rest of the day. Call me if it's important, otherwise I'll call in for messages later. Okay?"

"It's your lucky day. Not much is happening here;

it has been quiet."

"Pat, I may be out of the office tomorrow morning, too. I'm scheduled to meet with the FBI Agents on this matter." Pat reminded me that tomorrow I had numerous matters up for status call hearings. "Pat, call George Andrews at the D.A.'s office. Explain to him that I have a conflict and ask him for continuances. If he agrees, initiate calls to the judges' clerk for continuance dates."

My next call was to Special Agent Johns. "Mr. Johns, will the U.S. attorney's office prepare a proffer letter for me to review today? I will be working from my home. Let me give you that address, so your messenger can deliver the proffer for my signature. I will wait for it, and sign off today, if that's acceptable to you."

Rav was sipping a glass of water as I hung up the phone. His hands continued to shake as he asked, "What is a proffer letter?"

"It is an agreement with the United States attorney's office where the feds agree not to use it as the basis of a criminal charge, or use it as evidence at your trial, or anything that was disclosed to them at our meeting. That is unless your story changes or isn't truthful. But the government is free to use the information provided at a proffer for investigative leads."

"A proffer is not a grant of immunity, nor is it an agreement for a reduced sentence. It's possible the Feds are going after someone else and will want to offer you immunity or a deal for limited jail time at the meeting if you agree to be a cooperating witness."

I paused to allow the words sink in. "I tell all my clients that the proffer is not a 'get out of jail' card. If you tell the federal agents that you buried money under the apple tree, and tomorrow they start digging around the apple tree, they can use the evidence against you. So, be careful what you tell them tomorrow."

The U.S. attorney general at the time was Richard Gordon Kleindienst. Someone from the State Department told the U.S. attorney's office to instruct their people to go after Rabbi Lefkovitz on criminal charges. Someone from Nixon's inner circle had leaked a story that the Rav bribed a New York U.S. Congressman seeking favors.

The follow-up to the news article implied the Jewish establishment falsely used the plight of Soviet Jews as a fundraising tool, to enrich their financial coffers.

The Nixon administration sought to have Congress pass laws to make it illegal for not-for-profit organizations to pressure foreign governments. The Soviets were pleased by Washington's actions and thanked the Nixon administration.

The New York assistant U.S. attorney assigned to this case was Simon B. Schwartz. He was chosen for two reasons. First, he had a Jewish name, but was as secular as they came. Second, he had a reputation for being ruthless. Some say the 'B' in his middle name stood for 'bastard'. Simon and I attended Columbia Law School at the same time. Though he was a year ahead of me, we managed to attend a couple of the same classes. We didn't talk much back then, and we talked even less after graduation.

As a U.S. assistant attorney, he had an impressive history of obtaining convictions where powerful individuals were sentenced to long jail terms. Some witnesses later recanted their testimony, saying that Simon compelled and forced them to say things not true under duress. He had a reputation of playing it dirty and stretching legal ethics beyond acceptable limits. The only thing that mattered to Simon was the publicity of a conviction.

The Rav had to understand the type of man we would be facing in court, so I told him about Simon. "The story on the street is that his first wife filed for a divorce and when she came to domestic relations court, she had a black eye. When the judge asked, 'Mrs. Schwartz, what happened to your face'?

"She blurted out that it was her fault. 'Your honor, I failed to remind Simon of his son's birthday. I should have known better.'" The political weight of the Democratic Party was needed that day to preserve Simon's law license and career. The wife begged for the assault charge be dropped because she needed Simon's financial support.

I cooked the Rav an omelet as I asked him

questions. He interrupted me and asked me to call his wife. We phoned her several times during our interview process but there was no answer. I served him breakfast, but he wasn't eating as he worried about his wife's well-being.

# The scheme

After eating I pleaded with my father-in-law, "Rav, you need to talk to me. I must know everything there is to know. Don't withhold any details, no matter how unimportant it seems to you."

"Michael, my family came from a small village in Lithuania, not far from Vilna. I have a personal stake in helping our people emigrate from the U.S.S.R. to Israel or America where they can live and practice as Jews without the fear of reprisals. I established an organization that fulfills my mission to free our brothers and sisters."

"What's the name of this organization? What do they do? How do they accomplish their task?"

"The entity we established is called 'Exodus'. Monies I raise from my consulting are split fifty-fifty between the shul/yeshiva and Exodus."

"Who runs this program?"

"My son Yehuda is the accountant, and Mayer, the yeshiva's controller, oversees the day-to-day operations. I negotiate financial terms with Soviet government officials either on the telephone or in person. If necessary, either Yehuda and/or Mayer travel to Europe to finalize negotiations with these Communist government officials. Sometimes, the boys bring payments with them and turn it over to the trustee or the Soviet."

"The monies from Exodus are paid to another entity that we called Genesis. I think the majority of the payments to Soviet officials are paid by Genesis. In the beginning, I had to fly to Europe regularly to establish the connections. I believe the last time I was in Europe was the spring of 1970."

"What payments?" I felt like I was pulling teeth to extract details.

"Well…" He paused for a second. "In Europe and Russia, business is negotiated much differently than here. If I want hundreds of visas issued to release Soviet Jews, some of whom may be in Soviet prisons, a suitcase of money is required as a down payment. The balance is paid through a Swiss bank account transfer handled by Genesis once the refuseniks leave Russia, and land in Prague. It's all very simple. The process works."

"Once again. How does the money get to Europe and into whose Genesis's bank accounts?"

"We wire funds to a European trust bank account, in Genesis's name. The trustee of the Genesis trust makes payments to the Soviets." I noticed that his answer changed slightly. It was this type of inconsistency in the details that could have a jury question if he were telling the truth. It could mean the difference between freedom and jail time.

"Who runs this Genesis trust? Who are the owners of this foreign trust?"

"Genesis is owned by..." He paused before continuing. "I guess it is the yeshiva or me, I don't rightly remember. It's an entity formed on the island of Crete as a foreign corporation or a trust of some sort. The attorney thought this was the best way to conduct our business."

"Rav, tomorrow you will need to get me the paperwork showing who owns the two entities, so I can understand their legal formation in greater detail. It will be important for your credibility with a jury, if can recall all the facts. If you prefer, provide me the name of the attorney who established these entities, and I will contact him."

The Rav assured me, "I will try to find it, I'm sure it is in a file somewhere. On second thought, it may be quicker if you call Baruch Shinefield on Sixth Avenue. He was the attorney who handled these corporate matters."

I returned to asking operational questions of the Rav, "So, you wired funds to Genesis from Exodus. Who gives the Soviets the cash and who deposits the monies in the Swiss accounts?"

"Yehuda and Mayer wire the monies to Genesis as needed. On a rare occasion, they have hand delivered monies to Genesis. The trustee or a member of his staff will handle the banking details. He paused momentarily, "The process today is different from when we started two years ago. Now Yehuda and Mayer negotiate the terms and arrange for the visas on the telephone. If necessary, I will get involved on the call to negotiate the terms."

"If the Soviet official fears that they are being set-up, we calm their fears by setting up a personal meeting. In such instances, one or both boys fly to Europe to attend the meeting. Rarely, would Yehuda or Mayer carry cash, we do that for their safety. Usually, an employee of Genesis will hold the money offsite. Then, the trustee of the Genesis funds, Rabbi Isaac Azulay, establishes a Swiss bank account for the benefit of the Soviet official. Once Jews leave and land in Prague, the Russian official gets the numbers to the Swiss account."

"Can you trust Azulay?"

"He is beyond reproach. His family is one of the most respected families in Italy and Switzerland for the past five hundred years." The Rav took a couple of sips of tea. "From Prague, the Jewish Federation of New York assumes the financial burden for the refugees, providing funds for travel, food, shelter, medical and educational needs for their families."

"You mentioned securing U.S. visas. How do you obtain visas for these individuals?"

"John Boyle, the congressman from the seventeenth congressional district in Westchester, is a friend of our cause. He is the chairman of the subcommittee for immigration and border security. He arranges for the visas to be issued. We simply supply him with each person's name and personal information and his office completes the forms and he takes care of the rest."

"Didn't Boyle get indicted a couple of months ago for accepting bribes?"

"I really don't know."

"Have you paid him any monies?"

"To get the assistance we needed from him, we were asked to donate monies to his re-election campaign or to his various charities, so we wrote checks. That's how it works in every country."

The doorbell rang. I answered the call from the downstairs doorman. "Mr. Goldman, it's Marvin."

"Yes, Marvin."

"A messenger is here. Should I send him up?"

"Yes, please." It was the proffer being delivered.

I reviewed and read the details, signed the document, kept the second copy and gave the messenger the original and one copy to return to the feds. Between each sheet was a sheet of carbon paper. I had to press hard so my signature was legible on each page. I tossed carbon paper sheets in the garbage, there was no reason to keep them.

In the envelope, Simon wrote me a note and offered a deal, if the Rav pleaded guilty. The note said, 'Mr. Goldman, I appreciate that Rabbi Lefkovitz has retained an experienced and knowledgeable defense attorney. You do realize that your client could be facing forty to fifty years in prison. Because of our law school friendship, I offer you a deal if your client pleads guilty in the next forty-eight hours. The government will limit his prison sentence to seven years. I know you will do what's best for your client and his family'.

I gleaned from the note that, if necessary, Simon was willing to go after family members and destroy their lives to get a conviction. The second thing I surmised was that someone was pulling strings behind the scenes and they wanted a quick verdict otherwise they wouldn't have made such a sweet offer for a quick deal. I wished I could see the face of the puppet master behind the curtain as I gazed at the offer.

The Rav was impatient not hearing from his wife. He asked me to drive him to shul for afternoon services, and then to his home. I watched as he walked up the Shul's steps. Three religious men approached him and had words with him. The men spat on him, made offensive hand gestures while they yelled at him. I powered down the passenger side window long enough to hear the men yelling the word, "Gonif," (thief) as the Rav returned to my car. His eyes stared at the ground. His heart was broken.

In my car he said, "Michael, God is testing me. I must remain strong and faithful. God saves those who love him. However, God has a holy purpose, and we can't be expected to understand why things happen, even when bad tidings fall upon good people."

My mind questioned if he were talking to me or reassuring himself that he was innocent, and the heavens would protect him. During the two-minute ride to his apartment his eyes looked toward the heavens and his lips mumbled words intended only for our creator.

Stapled on the door to his apartment was a note that read: "Rabbi Lefkovitz, the board of directors has voted to terminate your employment. Pursuant to article seven, paragraph nineteen of your employment agreement, you have violated the morals clause of your contract. You will no longer be permitted unfettered access to the shul or the yeshiva. Our attorneys have advised us that we have the right to have you prosecuted if you trespass on the shul or yeshiva properties."

The note continued. 'Your personal belongings in your former office will be returned and delivered to your residence tomorrow. Finally, your residence is owned by the shul. This is your five-day legal notice demanding that you vacate the premises in the next seven days. After seven days, we will consider you a trespasser and will seek legal redress accordingly.'

Rav was so distraught, he handed me his keys to unlock the apartment door. Emah was sitting on the couch, weeping. The living room window had been shattered by a rock. The shattered glass fragments covered the floor and were embedded in the furniture. The Rav immediately went to his wife to console her. Emotionally, she was bruised, but she was unhurt by the pieces of glass. I said, "Rav, gather up your valuables and clothes. You will both sleep at my place until we can make other arrangements."

144

Rav and Emah carried out a small, locked metal box some clothing and personal items including texts. I carried two oversized suitcases down the stairs.

In the car, the Rav explained that being from the old country, he didn't fully trust banks. In the metal box was over twenty thousand dollars. The cash was his family's insurance that if a pogrom occurred here, they had sufficient funds to escape to Canada or elsewhere to start life over.

"Rav, this cash is a problem. If the feds learn of the existence of these funds, they will assume that you obtained them from illegal means. I strongly suggest that you gift these monies to Shira to hold in trust for you. If asked, by the government, don't tell them of its existence and be coy when discussing financial gifts to your children."

I added, "You never told me of these monies, and I will disavow any knowledge of their existence. We never had this conversation, otherwise I risk being disbarred." I didn't need to reassure him that Shira would return the monies once it was safe to do so. They had a special relationship that Rav didn't have with his other children.

In the car, my mind raddled with thoughts of how long my in-laws would be staying in our Manhattan home and what personal accommodations we would need to make to honor my in-laws' religious observances. When arrived at the condo, Shira and Ben were waiting as I opened the front door. Shira immediately went to hug her parents while she cried with her mother.

I gladly gave up my home office to her parents. The couch converted into an uncomfortable queen size bed until I could order a replacement bed to be delivered. The small closet wasn't sufficient for their clothes, so I made a mental note to purchase a dresser and nightstand.

With help from a friend, we moved my desk out of the bedroom and placed it in an alcove between the third bedroom and the living room. Afterwards, I had Shira call her siblings. We told them that the government might be investigating everyone in the family for money laundering. I explained that I needed a couple of days to sit with their parents to prepare their legal defense and would appreciate no visitors during this time.

I also had Shira warn the family. "Assume that the federal government has bugged your telephones, be careful what you say." I explained that anything they say on the phones could be misconstrued and used against them and their family in court. I pressed the point that they needed to be careful in all their communications even with people they know.

The Rav's two sons were afraid of social and economic repercussions and said they and their families wouldn't visit or call their parents until this affair had died down or had been resolved.

Yehuda had already been interviewed by the FBI and was afraid the yeshiva would terminate his employment. For all he knew, he could be called as a witness or a co-conspirator. The FBI demanded his cooperation. He told them that he knew nothing and as of that moment, he was sticking to that story.

I discussed the reaction from his sons with Rav. "My daughters have a stronger backbone than my sons. I understand their concerns. It's a small, closed Jewish community in Brooklyn. Yehuda fears his for his livelihood and the shunning of his wife and children. Yeshmel fears that the immigration authorities may challenge his wife's and her parents' immigration status. My son didn't want them to become casualties in this witch-hunt. I forgive each of my sons and I told them I understood."

Rav continued. "I worry that my arrest will embolden the Soviets' to punish our people even more so than they are already. We must win. Not for me, but for them!"

Emah was at an emotional loss. She was a fish out of water not knowing what to do and feeling helpless. Her friends now shunned her and instead of being active she was sitting idle on the couch watching television. Her sadness consumed her being. These were trying times; my condo was not made to host two families with different lifestyles.

I promised Shira that we would do whatever was needed so her parents felt comfortable and wanted.

# They weren't playing

I instructed Rav before meeting with the FBI, "Only answer the questions asked, keep your answers short and to the point. That means, do not explain your answers unless I ask you to do so. Answer the questions with a simple yes or no whenever possible. If the question requires more than a yes or no, provide a brief explanation. If I object to the question or if I tell you not to answer, stop talking until I tell you to resume. Do you understand?" He nodded his head, so after an hour-long session it was late so I called it quits so we could both could rest.

The next morning, Shira fed the Rav and me before we left and said she would pray for us. We cabbed over to the FBI headquarters. We walked into the federal building and were escorted up the elevator and into a windowless conference room with a rectangular wooden table and six dark, old, wooden chairs arranged around the table for our proffer meeting. We were directed to sit in the first two seats farthest from the door. The room was stuffy, and the lights were bright.

Across from us sat Simon Schwartz, the U.S. assistant attorney for the eastern district, Special Agent Johns from the FBI, and someone from the criminal division of the U.S. Treasury (the IRS). The U.S. attorney for the southern district of New York at the time had recused himself and Simon was placed in total control of the case. Another attorney took notes. It started out as a friendly meeting. A couple of jokes were exchanged before things became serious.

U.S. Assistant Attorney Schwartz read the Rav his Miranda rights. Johns asked the questions, reading them from the typed sheet he held in his hands. Each time Johns asked a question, Schwartz listened to the answer and made notes. The other attorneys made check marks or added notes on pads based on Rav's answers. Occasionally, one or more of the government's attorneys handed Johns a note requiring Johns to ask follow-up questions.

Johns started the second hour by asking questions related to Congressman Boyle. "Did you ever knowingly pay monies to U.S. House Representative John Boyle?"

"Yes, sir."

"How would you characterize these monies paid to Boyle? Why did you pay monies to him?"

"They were campaign donations," answered Rav.

"Were you aware that the monies you paid Boyle exceeded the campaign contribution limits permitted by law?"

"No. I mean, I didn't know that." Rav answered each question as we had rehearsed, calmly and in a normal speaking voice. I wished I'd had more time to properly prepare him, so the answers came across more polished.

"Why did you pay monies to Boyle in checks marked 'cash' or make checks payable to him personally?"

"I didn't do that, to the best of my knowledge." With each question, I was learning about possible violations that the government was pursuing. I needed to follow up on with my client once we returned to the condo.

"Did you run a business selling visas to illegal individuals here in the U.S.? Did you sell the visas supplied to you by Boyle?"

"No. I never sold any visas."

"What did you use the visas for?" Asked the frustrated agent. Rav explained the Russian connection and his work to save Jews but Johns was not buying it.

"Mr. Lefkovitz, what did you do with the tens of thousands of dollars in cash that you received from your charity?"

"I received perhaps three thousand dollars in cash a given year. However, I'm not quite sure of the exact amount. I never kept track of it. I receive these funds so I may distribute them to the poor, so they may buy food and pay rent."

By this time John's frustration was apparent as his voice became louder. "Mr. Lefkovitz, you have two business entities. Exodus is a Delaware corporation and Genesis an offshore trust. Do you deny having one or more of these entities pay you a sum of money exceeding one hundred thousand dollars annually? Do you deny transferring monies to foreign offshore bank accounts?"

I pointed my finger at Johns and said, "Excuse me, Special Agent Johns, don't take that tone with my client. Please afford him the respect he deserves and speak to him in a civil manner."

Johns looked at Simon who nodded. Then Johns said, "Forgive me, sometimes I get carried away."

Under control and unflustered, Rav answered, "None of your statements are true. I have not financially benefited from these entities."

Johns ignored Rav and asked, "Have you reported these ill-gotten monies on your personal income tax returns?"

"My income tax returns report all of my income to the best of my knowledge. I give the information to my tax preparer, Yehuda, my son and I sign them."

There were another twenty additional minutes of questions and denials and I could see the toll on Rav's face. I sat back and made notes. Unless the feds were bluffing, he would be facing a lengthy prison sentence, possibly twenty to forty years, if he lived that long. That was assuming the feds could prove their case.

The federal attorneys in the room thanked us after the meeting. Simon personally thanked me with a fake smile and a pat on the back. Today, reminded me of the Gingerbread Man story, who was assured by the alligator that nothing would happen to him. That is, until the alligator ate him. Then Simon asked if my client would be accepting the government's offer. I informed Simon that the offer was being respectfully rejected. Unbeknownst to me, the U.S. attorney's office presented their findings to a federal magistrate who determined that there was probable cause that Rav committed a federal crime. The government requested that a secret grand jury of between sixteen and twenty-three individuals be convened. The grand jury determined Rav was probably guilty of a federal crime and issued an indictment.

We were notified of the indictment a week later and I was permitted to surrender Rav in open court where he was given a detention and bail hearing. The prosecution read the charges to the defendant. I extended my father-in-law's plea on his behalf to the judge. "Rabbi Lefkovitz pleads not guilty." The judge advised us that Rav had a right to a jury trial. "Your honor, the defendant will exercise his rights to have a jury trial."

Judge Goodhammer responded, "Jury trial and the defendant pleads not guilty, correct?"

"Yes, Your Honor."

While we were in court at the detention and bail hearing, the feds raided and confiscated all Rav's and Emah's bank accounts, savings and retirement funds with an issued court order.

Rav's employer, the yeshiva without notice claimed he had violated the morals clause of his employment contract and therefore Rabbi Lefkovitz forfeited his retirement earnings. My in-laws were now penniless.

Judge Goodhammer had listened to the bail arguments at the detention hearing before ruling. The prosecutor demanded that my father-in-law be incarcerated as a flight risk or at a minimum be granted bail set at one million dollars. Knowing that he couldn't pay such a sum, I argued that Rabbi Lefkovitz was not a flight risk and was now unemployed with few financial resources. The judge knew that the FBI was confiscating the rabbi's monies during this hearing and ruled in our favor.

The judge looked at us and said, "I will permit Rabbi Lefkovitz to be released on his own recognizance based on the following negotiated government protections: he must surrender his passport, agree not to leave the State of New York without permission of this court and cease all immigrant visa activities without leave of the court. Does your client understand and agree to these conditions, Mr. Goldman?"

"Yes, Your Honor. Thank you!"

I surrendered Rav's passport to the attorney representing the government before we left court. During the argument phase of the prehearing before the judge, I personally vouched to the court that Rav would appear at trial and comply with the preconditions to his bail.

I knew the government wanted a quick trial and

verdict. We were granted ninety days for discovery, after which time the trial would begin, unless there was additional time required for discovery in the interest of justice.

I explained to Rav, "Discovery is where the prosecution is required to exchange all evidence they have gathered regarding this matter with the defense. This includes all evidence and information the government has obtained, regardless if it benefits their case or not. The feds must also turnover all the names of possible witnesses they may call at trial."

He nodded his head, so I continued. "The defense likewise shares with the prosecution all evidence the defense plans to introduce at trial including witness lists. The court may grant additional time for discovery if it is necessary." I paused to let all these legal terms and procedures sink in.

I was emphatic when I warned him. "We must stay vigilant I don't expect Simon to play fair. Some prosecutors like him violate legal ethics standards by destroying evidence that would benefit the defense's case or list possible witnesses that they have no expectation of calling at trial. The phony witness list is to force the defense to waste money, time and valuable resources preparing just in case these individuals are called to the stand."

To jump start our efforts, we initiated the litigation by preparing discovery schedules and potential witness lists. I learned after the detention hearing Rav's bank and retirement accounts were levied by the feds. The only way he could regain access these funds would be by winning at trial. A trial could be delayed for years.

I was already feeling claustrophobic in the condo and questioned how long I could survive under these conditions. I didn't have a place except the bathroom where I could have privacy.

Despite my worry, I tried to put things in perspective, I married my wife and knew there would be days like this. Up to now we lived a fairy tale existence and while things were tough on me, it was my wife who was emotionally suffering.

I had a client like Rav who had all his assets confiscated by the feds and was penniless. He had no other choice but to move his family into his parent's home. To increase the pressure on my client the feds threatened to charge his wife as a co-conspirator. Had he not agreed to plead guilty, his children could have been put into foster homes. Faced with these threats my client pleaded guilty on the trumped-up charges.

I worried Schwartz would go after Rav's family members in the hopes of having my father-in-law plead guilty to spare his family from possible incarceration. Yehuda worked at the yeshiva and was probably the likely choice to be his victim.

Rav put his trust in God and told me I was God's choice to combat the evil that he now faced. I was the one who felt pressured to win for the sake of the cause but mostly for my wife.

Late that evening, after preparing Rav for trial, I changed the conversation and asked, "Rav, Shira shared with me that Yeshmel's wife Deena is Russian, and you procrastinated in blessing her marriage to Yeshmel. I'm curious; why did you wait so long before you allowed Yeshmel to marry her? If you don't mind me asking."

"Michael, she is Latvian, not Russian. Deena came to the yeshiva one day to express her gratitude for my efforts in freeing her family. Her father was a doctor and refusenik. While I met with her, she asked if she could assist Exodus and work for us. At first, I was worried that she might be a Soviet plant to disrupt our efforts, but I permitted the controller to hire her.

"While she was working one night, Yeshmel came into the office where she worked and the two met. Yeshmel was immediately taken by her. He couldn't study, and..." Rav giggled. "My son was consumed with lust and she was constantly on his mind. He was addicted to her and couldn't pass her door without poking his head in the doorway and have an extended conversation.

Eventually, he asked if I would go to the matchmaker to arrange for them to see each other — chaperoned of course. I granted him my permission to proceed. I didn't tell him that I needed to look into her soul first before I'd allow them to marry. Was her beauty only skin deep? I had many questions, but I didn't tell him my concerns. I made it a point to have discussions with Deena during the day at work. I learned that she was an ethical, caring woman who would be a good wife to my son. I eventually blessed them getting married.

"Michael, I knew from the first time we spoke you had a righteous soul and a good heart. Your love for my daughter was apparent. Besides, Shira has my instinct or ability to read the souls of others. She told me that you were her bashert. Who was I to contradict her?"

As he said that I recalled times when Shira offered me advice and it was uncanny that she was able to solve problems that I had been working on for weeks. We would meet people and right away she had a sense of whether they could be trusted. It was true Shira had a special God-given gift. Some would call it premonitions; others would say it's an inner voice that warns you if there is danger.

Rav's mood appeared steady and resolute which gave me hope that he would be able to stand up to the rigors of a trial.

# I wasn't planning for this

Meanwhile, four months passed since Rav was initially charged and my home life became unbearably miserable. There was no room where I could have peace and quiet. Emah was in the kitchen or the living room, Ben's toys were scattered throughout the apartment. Every night Shira's sisters and grandchildren would come to visit, and I felt like the 'old woman who lived in a shoe, she had so many children she didn't know what to do'.

Shira did her best as a wife, daughter and mom. She was there to console her mom, attend to Ben, study her college courses and entertain our guests. I could tell she was overwhelmed and depressed. Yet, she didn't complain though, I noticed my wife's smile had disappeared. More times than not, she stared at an empty coffee cup, she too was at her breaking point.

We rarely had time for ourselves. Instead of date night, Shira chose to stay home and babysit her parents. Her devotion and love for her parents was commendable, but it put a strain on our relationship.

Because of my mounting frustration, I took refuge in my office and chose to work late most evenings. I didn't want to be home in the midst of turmoil. I rationalized that it gave me an opportunity to earn money working on paying clients' matters. The quiet of my office at night was my escape. I installed a television and at night watched sports and quietly relaxed with a cold beer.

Don't get me wrong, it also wasn't easy for Rav or Emah. Emah seemed lost; she didn't know what to do with her time. She sat in a chair in front of the television or sat on a park bench talking to herself. Shira tried to snap her mom out of her funk by taking her for walks or shopping just to get her out of the apartment. But it seemed nothing helped; she was immersed in self-pity.

Emah was depressed and eventually the doctors prescribed an antidepressant: Imipramine and then Valium to help her sleep. All their household belongings, books and keepsakes were placed in storage lockers. They had little to no access to their belongings which added to their frustration. Rav and Emah found life in Manhattan strange and unwelcoming and their smiles disappeared.

At night, I had the time to begin working on Rav's case in earnest. During the discovery period, I finally got my hands on copies of the feds' evidence. The prosecution provided me with checks, documents, pictures, affidavits and everything else they had collected.

It was my job as his attorney to debunk each of the criminal charges the government claimed if I hoped to keep Rav out of prison. The evidence seemed overwhelming as I initially reviewed the documents. The criminal complaint spelled out facts to support all the charges in the government's case. I had Ariel from my office assist me in preparing our defense by running down leads, interviewing witnesses and verifying evidence. This trial was becoming a media circus with the feds leaking erroneous stories to the press.

The leaks to the newspapers generated negative news articles which were biased against my client. The impact of the bad publicity caused Emah and Rav to experience further alienation among their few remaining friends and the Jewish community. I filed a court motion to suppress the Fed's leaks.

At the pretrial, I successfully argued that the feds were responsible for the leaks and asked the court to issue a gag order. It was a small victory. The celebration was short-lived as the trial date was approaching.

# Monies paid to Boyle

I examined the evidence relating to each charge in the complaint. The feds provided me with the following documents and evidence which they planned to introduce to convict Rabbi Lefkovitz at trial.

1. A sampling of fifty-five checks paid to Boyle from Rav where the payee was either Boyle or cash. Rav was the check signer either by hand or with a facsimile stamp. Typed in the memo section of the checks were the individual payees' names. None of these names were Russian sounding.

2. There was a potential witness list of twenty individuals who allegedly would swear that Rav negotiated payments to supply them with visas or green cards.

3. Checks or cashier's checks payable to cash. The witnesses who would claim the payments were paid to Rav for visas. The actual number of individuals receiving visas allegedly surpassed one hundred. Each person supposedly paid Rav three thousand dollars or more.

4. Boyle had been convicted of taking bribes and money laundering earlier in the year. He was willing to testify against Rav in the hopes that his cooperation

would earn him leniency when the court ruled on his prison sentence.

5. From the secretary of state's office, a list of individuals for whom the congressman requested special consideration, green cards or visa actions. This list had many of the witnesses listed to testify against Rav.

6. Lists of names from Boyle's office citing individuals for whom Rav requested visas.

7. Banking information, deposit slips and copies of deposits reflecting the checks paid to Boyle from one of Rav's related entities including the yeshiva.

8. Checks cashed at currency exchanges paid by the yeshiva, bearing Rav's signature stamp or his personal signature.

9. Checks paid from the yeshiva to Exodus.

10. Copies of the yeshiva's general ledgers with accounting entries for cash payments paid to Rav with the notation: 'helping the poor'.

I looked through the mountain of evidence and considered the case hopeless. I visualized my father-in-law wearing stripes while serving prison time. On the surface, the government appeared to have a compelling case. On its face this evidence could easily sway a jury of his guilt beyond a reasonable doubt. It was my job to poke holes in their case, so a jury would acquit my client.

I sat with Rav and had him examine each check. He verified both his signature and said the signature stamp appeared authentic. But he didn't recall seeing the immigrants' names typed in the memo section of the checks when he signed the payments payable to Boyle. It was impossible to determine when the memo section were filled in, before or after the checks were signed.

The handwritten signatures were most problematic. Someone on the jury would expect Rav to have reviewed the checks before he signed them. Fortunately, most of the checks were signed by use of a signature stamp. Rav grew sad, shed a tear or two and looked despondent as he held the checks between his fingers. He mumbled something to himself and when I asked, he told me it didn't matter. He now realized he had been too trusting.

To complicate matters, when I examined the checks and the cashier's check copies of the immigrant payments, I found that they were not deposited into the yeshiva account, it appeared the monies had been cashed at one of four currency exchanges in New York. The endorsement on these checks bore Rav's name.

I was beginning to see signs of trouble and grew suspicious. I pondered if my client had the wherewithal to create such an elaborate, complicated criminal operation. It wouldn't be the first or the last time this question surfaced in my brain as I prepared to do battle. In the back of my mind, I had to consider if Rav knew more than he was sharing with me. When it comes to lawyer/client relations, that dynamic can sink a ship even before it sets sail.

# Three weeks before the trial

A dark cloud continued to hang over my home. My wife's depression, mostly due to her mother's mental deterioration. Shira and I tried but nothing snapped Emah out of her funk. The doctors told us that in time the medications would cure her. In the meanwhile, the pills kept Emah smiling but in a state of fantasy, unable to deal with reality.

My wife was stressed with school, our son, and caring for her folks. She was short-tempered with me and expected me to do more than I was doing. I was over-whelmed working long hours without a normal home life.

Our sex life had soured. My wife was apprehensive when I initiated sex. When I brought up the question of sex, Shira would whisper, "Michael! My parents are awake in the next room; now is not an appropriate time." Or she might have said, "Michael I'm exhausted; I'm sorry, can you wait for Friday night?" I was sexually and emotionally frustrated. My home felt like a boarding house and I needed some tender loving care. I wanted my life back to the way it was.

Even the Yankees' 1972 season sucked. They were playing five hundred baseball and were sitting in fourth place. Ron Blumberg, the Jewish ballplayer, dubbed the next Mikey Mantle, couldn't hit. I couldn't even listen to games on the radio at home because either our son was sleeping, or her parents were resting.

Finally, I called my mom and drove out to Long Island. She greeted me at the door. "Son, why are you so glum?" I proceeded to tell her everything. I was going to explode if I didn't talk to someone. I needed her advice. "Michael, when was the last time the two of you got away for a few days alone?"

"Never. We have never taken a vacation or a honeymoon. We had Ben right away and family responsibilities kept us from getting out of town."

"You need to get away."

"Mom, the trial is in three weeks, we have Ben and…" Before I could finish my sentence, I began to shake my head and started to cry out of sheer frustration as I clenched my fists.

Mom grabbed my arm. "Your wife sounds like she too needs time off. She needs a vacation from the stress she is experiencing. I'm not sure if you have been there when she needed your help. Like your father, it was too easy to run away, leaving her to deal with all the family's problems. It sounds like you are responsible for destroying your marriage!"

I was shocked by her response. It was a cold bucket of water thrown at me. I didn't expect her cutting words. I had considered myself the victim. Almost shouting at her because my nerves were shot, I said, "So, what is

165

your solution?"

"Use my phone and call Kutsher's Hotel. See if you can book a reservation for next week. Carol and I will take turns watching Ben here at my place."

Kutsher's was an all-inclusive kosher hotel in the Catskill Mountains offering recreation, relaxation and an evening entertainment program. In its day, Dean Martin, Louis Armstrong and Woody Allen had all performed there. Famous heavyweight boxers once trained there too. The hotel was less than one hundred miles northwest of Manhattan, so it was easy to reach.

I returned home and told Shira about the plans I made and the reservations I booked. "For the sake of our marriage, we need to go!" I was emphatic.

"Michael, we'll take a vacation after the trial. I just finished my finals; I will have more time now and it will be less stressful. Besides, how can I leave my parents?"

"Shira, they're adults! We leave them alone most days as it is. I need to get away from all this. We have not gotten away, just the two of us since Ben was born, we need to now! Bottom line: next week, I will go with or without you."

"Michael, you're not being fair." With that I turned my back, walked away from her and took a shower. I was too angry to fall asleep. I wound up tossing and turning. My blood pressure must have been spiking.

The next morning, I purposefully left for work earlier than normal because I didn't want to talk to Shira. I was talking to myself as I stood to board the subway. I readied myself to push my body into the crowded commuter car to physically release my aggressions. Once in the train car, the body odors were overwhelming. I prayed I could hold my breath until the subway reached my destination. My mind was consumed with self-pity and I still wanted to explode.

Shira woke and walked into the kitchen. She looked for me, instead she saw her father in the living room reading the paper and wished him a good morning. Shira then began the routine of preparing breakfast for her parents and Ben before leaving for school. Rav joined her in the kitchen. He stroked his beard as he asked, "How are you doing?"

With a slight smile, she said, "Wonderful. I'm truly blessed with an incredible son and husband."

"Shira, the Talmud tells us that family and relations between a husband and wife are holy. It is the duty of both the husband and wife to please the other and satisfy their spiritual and emotional needs. How can you be happy if your spouse isn't?"

"Aba, did Michael have words with you? Did he?" Her voice seemed strained from the stress she was under.

"Shira, he said nothing to me except legal matters regarding the trial."

"Aba, we were thinking of going away next week for a few days. Would you mind?"

"Of course not. Go enjoy yourselves. God bless you two."

A few moments later, I received a call at the office as I was getting my desk situated. Pat said, "Its Shira." I thanked her and reluctantly picked up the telephone.

Sarcastically, I said, "Yes, dear."

"I'm packing my bags. I am going to Gimbles and will pick up a swimsuit today. I hope I can find something that fits. Do you need anything while I'm there?"

My heart was filled with joy as I said, "You made me so happy. I love you! Thank you!" My voice carried throughout the office suite.

All week I thought about nothing but the trip. I worked with Pat and the staff to cover all my matters, so there would be nothing to worry about. At night, all I could talk about with Shira was the hotel's amenities and layout.

At long last, our getaway day arrived. The music played in the background as we drove to the hotel. As we sang along with the radio, I joked that it was to the week, three years ago Ben was conceived just a few miles away from this very hotel. Shira changed the mood by expressing concern for Ben and her parents who we left behind.

I begged her, "Please, for the next four days, let's pretend we are on an island with no telephones and no worries. Let's pretend we are entirely carefree with no problems hanging over our heads. Let's relax and renew our love for each other. Oh yes, let's have great sex."

"I guess I have neglected you over the past couple

of months. I promise to make it up to you."

We checked in, went to our room and dressed to join the hundreds of other vacationers around the Olympic-sized, outdoor swimming pool. We ordered lemonades and a light lunch. As we sat on lounge chairs under a cloudless blue sky, we soaked up the sun's rays, totally blissed out.

Being outside and away from work and the related stress was liberating. I jumped in the pool, lowered my swim goggles and began swimming laps in one of the lanes dedicated for adult swimmers. Shira started a new romance novel. She hadn't had time to read one since her father was indicted.

I swam thirty laps, returned from the water and lay on the lounger next to Shira. Now refreshed, with a smile on my face, I leaned over to her as she read and asked, "What do you want to do tomorrow? She put down her book, marking the page and looked at me with eyes that said, why are you interrupting my reading? I'm enjoying the peace and quiet. Can't it wait until later?

Having visited Kutsher's with my parents during the summers growing up, I knew my way around, but it was her first time. "Michael, I can just lie on this chair and read for the next two days. To me, that would be a perfect vacation. However, I see that twinkle in your eye. What do you want to do tomorrow?"

Gleefully I responded. "Glad you asked! Tomorrow, if you agree, we can take a four-mile hike and climb up to the Katterskill falls along the Spruce

Creek. Or we can take the car and walk from the parking lot up to the waterfalls. Then, I would like to spend the day going on some easy hiking trails. There is great scenery to see, and it will be just the two of us."

"If it makes you happy, I'm in, but promise me two days from now, I get a day at the pool, just to read before we return to our mayhem. Okay?"

"Yes, dear."

"Let's take the car. I will have the hotel pack sandwich lunches for us. Michael is there anything else that I should take care of before we set forth on our excursion?"

We laid by the pool for hours. The sun drained the energy from our bodies. We re-entered our room, showered, set the alarm clock and enjoyed a nap before dinner. In the hotel dining room, we shared a table with another couple and their two delightfully obnoxious children. The little monsters spilled their chocolate milk across the table at us and threw food at each other. After dinner, I whispered to Shira, "I hope our kids are never like this."

We returned to the room and when Shira turned to ask me about the hotel's evening entertainment options, I pushed her against the wall and passionately kissed her. We ended up on the bed as I began to take her clothes off. Shira started to say something, but I stopped her. "Please dear, not now. Tell me later."

Driven by hormones, there was little foreplay, and the lovemaking was intense. I needed and wanted unrestrained sex to release all my pent-up frustrations. I wanted to enjoy myself without worrying about disturbing anyone in the next room. After I climaxed, my sweaty body rested on hers. I took a deep breath and closed my eyes. She smiled knowing how badly we both needed this.

Having my needs satisfied and in a relaxed post-sex state of mind, I asked, "Shira, what was it you wanted to tell me before we had sex?"

She laughed. "Michael, before we started, I wanted to tell you that my diaphragm was in my suitcase."

I laughed. "I guess it's too late now. Is this a fertile time of the month for you?"

"Very."

"Oops. Let's make sure that we made a baby the first time." With that, I rolled her over and started fondling her breasts with my tongue as my fingers played with her inner thigh. She smiled. I don't think she was planning to get pregnant on this trip, but she didn't protest.

The next morning, we awoke in fantastic moods following an evening of lovemaking. Even our appetites had improved. After breakfast, we grabbed the prepared lunch basket from the kitchen and headed to the falls.

The waterfalls, rivers and vistas were picturesque. Our four days at Kutsher's were marked with luscious food and great sex. We also renewed our love for one another and regretted having to return to Manhattan. The diaphragm never made it out of her suitcase.

Before we returned home Friday morning, we picked Ben up from my mom's and thanked her. Mom couldn't stop telling us how she loved the time with her grandson and wanted to tell us all the cool things they did while we were gone.

While I was gathering up Ben's stuff, Mom told us that Ben helped bake cookies and cakes. Of course, he volunteered to lick the spoon and taste test the baked goods. We buckled Ben into the car seat and drove home. Grandma gave him two cookies to eat on the ride home. This kid was on a sugar high for the next two days from all the treats he ate.

Rav was overjoyed to see Ben as we arrived home. He held him as they sang and talked together for countless hours. Ben missed him too. Playing and holding Ben was his way of forgetting his troubles. They shared a special relationship that Ben would recall all his life.

Looking back, I'm convinced Shira and I also survived these dark times because we had Ben in our lives. Playing in the park and reading stories to him helped us to temporarily forget the harsh realities we were living through.

# The case against the Rav continues

Nearly half a million dollars were deposited into the Exodus bank accounts annually. The check registers and bank statements from the yeshiva indicated that checks to Boyle were made payable to cash. These monies totaled about six thousand dollars per month for the past thirty-six months. The government told us that there was six thousand dollars received by the yeshiva every month from illegal immigrants and these were cashed at currency exchanges.

The currency exchange employees were government witnesses who allegedly agreed to testify that Rav personally cashed the checks made payable to cash. When we interviewed the potential government witnesses and showed them pictures of Rav, they recanted their stories. Collectively, they didn't recognize the man in the photograph. The case just got more complicated, because I knew someone else at the yeshiva perpetrated the fraud. Could it be Yehuda?

The trial date had arrived, and we now had to choose a jury. We had to choose a jury from a pool of approximately one hundred individuals which included a mixture of young, old, blacks, whites, Hispanics and a couple of Asians. The jury pool consisted of a true cross section of New Yorkers.

I conferred with Ariel, my co-counsel as we developed a profile of jurors, we felt would be most favorable to our defense. The list included naturalized citizens because they would appreciate the extent to which Rav went to help others in obtaining visas. They might even be willing to overlook the bribes of Russian officials as a necessary evil.

We also wanted religious people on the jury, hoping they might see Rav as doing God's work. The biggest challenge was to weed out those who hated Jews.

To start the jury selection process, the judge asked if there were any individuals who couldn't physically or emotionally serve as jurors. Then he asked whether serving would cause an undue hardship. If the individual had a valid excuse, the judge dismissed them from their jury obligations. As long as the judge found an individual to be of sound mind and body to sit on the jury, they were eligible to serve.

After some prospective jurors were dismissed, the remaining prospective jurors were scrutinized by the judge. He would ask questions of potential jurors in a process known as 'voir dire', which is a French phrase that means 'to speak the truth'.

The purpose of this line of questioning was to discover if a potential juror had personal biases which could influence their rendering of a decision. We inquired into their backgrounds and sometimes family histories. Each side was permitted to have a potential juror excused without providing a reason to the court.

It took three days to select our jury and jury alternates. Alternates were individuals who were available to replace a juror who might be excused during the trial. We had six jurors with whom we considered possibly sympathetic of our client and others who could go either way.

The jury members were impaneled and sworn in by the judge, the Honorable Jack D. Weinberg. He was the federal court judge for the Eastern District of New York, who would preside over the trial. Simon Schwartz was the prosecuting attorney for the United States government.

Judge Weinberg had been on the bench for the past three years and though I had never appeared before him, the talk on the street was that he was a no-nonsense fair judge. He had a reputation for having a dry sense of humor, who occasionally delivered humorous anecdotes from the bench.

Schwartz, my opposing counsel, couldn't be trusted, but I pretended to be his friend when we chatted. I had to hide my disdain for him for the sake of my client.

The courtroom was filled to capacity with onlookers and press. Judge Weinberg sat in his traditional black robe, a gavel in his right hand, high above the spectators. Both the stars and stripes and the New York state flag were positioned on either side of him. The mood on the street and the press wasn't favorable to our side. The majority of the people wanted Rav found guilty of misusing donated funds entrusted to him.

Judge Weinberg motioned Simon to begin his opening arguments. Simon walked up to the jury box and faced the jury. He paused for a couple of seconds as he stared each juror in the eye. Simon appeared to the jury as a man of normal build, shy of six feet and clean-shaven. He wore a Hart Schaffner and Marx designer black suit with thin white stripes. His bright red, silk handkerchief was folded into a pocket square ever so neatly in his upper suit pocket. A red power tie and Oxford black shoes completed his appearance. Even his fingernails had been neatly manicured.

Simon hoped to ignite passion amongst the jury members with his opening remarks. He posed a question to the jury. "Who do you see sitting in the defendant's chair?" He paused for a couple of seconds. "Do you think we would be prosecuting a religious man for noble acts of charity?" He paused again and shook his head in disgust, as he pointed his index finger at Rav. "We will present evidence that this man embezzled hundreds of thousands of dollars using dummy corporations that he organized here in the United States and overseas."

Simon paused for effect and continued. "Don't you find it despicable when someone hides behind the cloak of helping the poor while they are only lining their own pockets with money? In fact, this man raised money on the pretense of saving the world from the Soviet threat. He is a real-life Mafia godfather just like in the movies and—"

I stood up and loudly interrupted Simon's remarks. "I object, Your Honor. 'The Godfather' is a fictional character currently at the movie theaters who threatened and murdered individuals. The good rabbi here saved people's lives. He didn't kill them."

The judge agreed with my objection. "Objection sustained. The jury should ignore any reference to 'The Godfather'. The Rabbi has not performed any acts that resemble the actions performed of any fictional character in the 'Godfather' movie. Please continue, Mr. Schwartz."

"By the end of this trial, you will have heard from scores of witnesses pointing the finger of guilt at that man, Rabbi Lefkovitz. Then, you will have the obligation to find this charlatan guilty for the crimes he committed." Simon pointed again at my father-in-law. "Send a loud message to those who misuse and steal charitable funds, like Rabbi Lefkovitz, show him that New York punishes and imprisons its criminals!"

Murmurs were heard throughout the courtroom, prompting a pounding of the judge's gavel to restore order.

Simon then turned to the judge. "Your Honor, I have concluded my opening remarks."

It was my turn to deliver my opening remarks. I began educating the jury that Rav had a long history of performing charitable deeds and the civic work. "Rabbi Lefkovitz is a family man, devoted to his wife of over forty-two years. He has five children and many grandchildren. He is revered in his community and a notable world-renowned scholar."

The rabbi received cash monies from his charities. These monies were distributed to the poor. Rabbi Lefkovitz provided the disadvantaged with meals, shelter and clothing. He took no personal benefit from the cash entrusted to him." I paused to allow the jury to consider what I had said.

"When the FBI took possession of the rabbi's life savings, they found the rabbi's bank accounts amassed less than fifty thousand dollars representing over forty years of work. A bell should have gone off alerting the FBI that they had the wrong man. This is a man who raised over half a million dollars a year for charitable causes and had a fraction of that in savings and lived a blue-collar lifestyle. Rabbi Lefkovitz drove an old Plymouth Fury and lived a modest life in a Brooklyn apartment that he didn't own. His life's work was to serve others and to make the world a better place."

I walked deliberately along the length of the jury box, stroking my right hand on my chin before I spoke again. "Rabbi Lefkovitz saved countless Russian Jews by supplying them with visas. To acquire these visas, Rabbi Lefkovitz drew on support from an elected official. When asked, the rabbi and his institutions donated monies to support the re-election campaign of the congressman in question."

"At no time did Rabbi Lefkovitz know that it was illegal to donate funds to a re-election campaign. At no time did the congressman limit the amount of donations or tell the rabbi that there were federal campaign laws limiting donations." My goal was to acknowledge rather than hide from the most damaging evidence and turn it to a positive.

After I finished my opening remarks, the judge asked, "Do you wish to call your first witness, Mr. Schwartz?"

"Yes, Your Honor, I wish to call—"

Just then, Shira came running into the courtroom bawling hysterically. I looked back as I heard the commotion and unexpectedly saw my wife. She flung herself into my arms. Her tears smacked me in the face. "Emah's dead!" The news shocked both me and Rav so powerfully, we were lost for words.

In disbelief, Rav stood up; his mouth remained wide open, and tears flowed as he tried to make sense of this surreal news.

The judge slammed his gavel down several times demanding an end to the courtroom commotion. I looked at the judge. "Your Honor, may I approach the bench?" The judge nodded. Simon stood next to me in front of the bench. "Your Honor, it appears the rabbi's wife has died. I request a two-week recess, so we may plan for her interment and permit the rabbi to sit shiva."

Having both a Jewish judge and prosecutor was a

blessing. I didn't need to explain that the rabbi would be observing the seven days of mourning after the funeral.

"Mr. Goldman, your request for a two-week recess is immediately granted. Court is adjourned." Before we could turn to the exit the judge added, "Mr. Goldman and Rabbi Lefkovitz, the court wishes to express its sympathy to you and the entire Lefkovitz family at this time." We were too emotionally overwhelmed to utter a word. I just nodded and turned to leave the court while embracing Shira.

We later learned Emah had taken her Imipramine that morning. Feeling the stress of the first day of the trial, she took an extra two doses. As the medicine kicked in, she opened the sliding glass doors and stepped out to the balcony. There she knelt on the chair and leaned over to the railing until she fell to the pavement below.

The sun had been in her eyes and noise from the traffic below filled the air. The sound of her body crashing onto the sidewalk below startled all in the vicinity. The Imipramine had given her the confidence that she was capable of flying. Her blood splattered on the pavement, on the walls of our building and the cars parked below. Thankfully, she died immediately, according to the EMTs who were called to the scene.

The funeral was attended by family, friends of Emah, Rav Shira and mine. Two reporters attended the ceremony attempting to write a human-interest story about her tragic death.

It was a cloudy day and the fog hampered visibility. A close rabbinical friend of Rav conducted the graveside ceremony. Neither a bird nor airplane interrupted the service. The silence of the cemetery was broken only by the words of the rabbi. Emah was buried in a traditional pine box with no metal fittings. Family members carried the casket to the plot.

After the ceremony, the family filled the grave with dirt, keeping with centuries-old Jewish tradition. Ben instinctively hugged his grandfather during the entire burial and Rav held on to him for dear life.

The shiva was attended by guests from my office, friends and family. Shira and her sisters shared tales of Emah's virtues, as they cried and held each other. We received numerous food trays graciously sent from numerous friends.

There was so much food, I begged guests and condo employees to take some of it home. For seven nights, Sara and a couple of other close friends stayed late after the guests left and assisted us in the clean-up. I spent every night, after everyone had left, holding Shira in my arms as she tried to reconcile what had happened. Rav looked to the heavens and searched to find answers while appearing emotionally strong for the sake of his children.

It was queer; one day during the shiva Rav looked at me and said, "King David once said to God, 'I would rather be punished by you than at the cruel hands of man'." Then he returned to his room hoping to find answers in a religious book.

I pondered his words and assumed he was referring to the trial. If he committed a sin God would be more merciful with his punishment than having it administered by someone like Simon Schwartz.

After the shiva period ended, Rav attended the morning and evening services at the neighborhood orthodox shul. He prayed for his wife and kept to himself and didn't allow others to socialize with him. The shock of his wife's death had caught him off guard. He questioned himself mercilessly, wondering whether he did enough to support Emah while she was alive. Every day he punished himself, second guessing if he bore responsibility for her death.

# The trial resumes

Now after Emah's death, I was representing a defendant who didn't care if he lived or died. I asked him questions pertinent to the case and found him to be non-responsive. Some might say that without the defendant's input my case was a lost cause. He only seemed attentive when Ben was present. When Ben ran into his arms, my father-in-law's eyes lit up and his heart beat with vigor. Mourning is a gradual process, but we had a trial that would be resuming, and I needed him to focus.

Unfortunately, Rav spent his hours day and night in his room reading religious texts. He sat down with us for meals, but his mind was distracted and didn't respond when asked questions except those asked by Ben.

Nevertheless, the two weeks quickly passed, and the trial resumed. Simon called his first witness. "The prosecution calls Ivan Calderon." Calderon was sworn in by the clerk of the court and sat in the witness box to the right of the judge and directly in front of the government's table.

Sitting alongside me at our table was Ariel, my co-counsel and next to him Rav who read religious texts.

The jury was seated closest to the government's table and nearest to the witness box. Behind the prosecution and defense attorney's table stood a two-foot-high dark walnut divider separating us from the courtroom observers. In the two rows behind us sat Rav's daughter and some grandchildren, providing moral support.

A lean man in his mid-fifties, Calderon settled into the witness chair. "Mr. Calderon," Simon said, "please state your full name, address and profession." Calderon wore a blue, patched, worn-out worker's uniform along with muddy, old work boots. His unshaven face was sun-beaten and weathered.

"Ivan Calderon. I am a gardener and I live in the Bronx," he said in a heavy accent.

"Mr. Calderon, do you have a green card and does that card permit you to remain and work in this country?"

"Yes."

"Mr. Calderon, how or where did you acquire your green card?"

"I paid for it."

"From whom did you purchase it?"

"From Rabbi Lefkovitz." The jurors and the onlookers stared at Rav.

"How did you learn of Rabbi Lefkovitz?"

"A friend of mine told me that he sells green cards."

"How much did you pay the rabbi?"

"Three thousand dollars."

"Cash?"

"No, cashier's checks. Four of them."

"How did you deliver the cashier's checks to the rabbi?"

"I mailed the money to the Post Office box number I was given, along with forms that needed to be completed."

"Here in my hand are four cashier's checks. Do you recognize them?"

"Yes. These are the checks that I used to pay for the green card."

"Are these cashier's checks payable to the rabbi? Did you send them to the rabbi?"

"Yes, these were my cashier's checks in the amount of seven hundred and fifty dollars each. I mailed each one to the rabbi."

"Your Honor, I would like to admit these four checks into evidence. They have been marked government's exhibits one hundred and twenty-three through number one hundred and twenty-six."

The judge asked, "Are there are any objections?"

I responded by saying, "No objections, Your Honor."

The judge said, "So moved."

Simon picked up a note pad and examined it before continuing with his examination. "Mr. Calderon, to what address did you mail your checks?"

"I mailed all the checks to Post Office box 666, Brooklyn, New York."

"Your Honor, at this time, the government would

like to tender into evidence a notarized letter from the manager at this post office certifying that Post Office Box 666 belongs to the Bol Shuva Yeshiva. I want to mark this as government's exhibit one hundred and twenty-seven."

"Do you have any objections, Mr. Goldman, to the admission of this document into evidence?"

I stood. "For the record, Mr. Schwartz failed to properly set the foundation for this document. However, I have no objection."

The judge said, "So moved. Mr. Schwartz, in the future, please follow proper protocols for the introduction of evidence."

Simon nodded his head and returned to questioning the witness. "Mr. Calderon, did you receive your green card from the rabbi?"

"No. I received it in the mail, from Washington D.C., the capital."

"Was it mailed by the United States Department of Immigration?"

"Yes."

"Your witness." Simon returned to the government's table and sat down.

I approached the witness with a smile on my face. "Mr. Calderon, have you ever met with Rabbi Lefkovitz before today? The rabbi is seated there, at the table do you recognize him?" My index finger pointed at Rav.

"No, sir."

"How do you know that it was this rabbi who sold

you the green card?"

"He told me that was his name." There were a few chuckles from the onlookers.

"These are the cashier's checks that you paid to the rabbi, correct?"

"Yes."

"Whose name is on the cashier's check as the payee on each of the cashier's checks?"

"Cash."

"Is cash the rabbi's nickname?" A few snickers were again heard from the gallery before the judge silenced the commotion.

Schwartz objected, and I withdrew my last question.

"Mr. Calderon, you testified that you spoke to the rabbi. Was that face-to-face or on the telephone?"

"On the telephone."

"On the telephone. Huh, was the voice on the phone that of a younger or older man?" The witness hesitated and looked at Simon before answering. I pounced on his failure to respond to my question.

"Mr. Calderon, why are you looking at Mr. Schwartz for the answer to my question? Did Mr. Schwartz or one of his attorneys tell you what to say today?"

"Uh." The entire court witnessed Calderon looking for assistance before answering the question. As the judge was instructing the witness to answer the question, Simon quickly jumped to his feet. "I object,

Your Honor, at the insinuation that Mr. Goldman has invoked that I coached this witness."

The judge immediately took charge and said, "Approach the bench, Counselors. The court, at this time, will take a ten-minute break. Mr. Calderon, you are not permitted to talk with anyone, or any party involved in these proceedings during this break. Do you understand my instructions?" Calderon nodded his head, to which the judge replied, "Good."

I joined the judge and Simon in the judge's chambers. The judge lifted his glasses and said, "Mr. Schwartz, did your witness receive assurances that his green card would not be revoked, and his immigration status would not be voided if he testified today?"

There was a pause as Judge Weinberg awaited a response. Schwartz answered, "Yes."

"Did you assist your witness with his testimony for today's proceedings?"

"Yes, Your Honor. Being new to our country, I had to properly prepare him for the court hearing."

"Did you tell Mr. Goldman that you had an arrangement or a deal with the witness?"

"I don't recall, Your Honor."

"Did you make similar arrangements or deals with all the witnesses testifying about their permanent visa and green card status?"

"Your Honor, the witnesses fear deportation. Assuring them that their status was not in jeopardy was the only way I could get the witnesses to come forward and testify without fear."

"Mr. Schwartz, I will assume there was no intentional witness tampering. If I find out there has been, there will be serious repercussions. Do we understand each other?" Simon nodded his head in agreement.

The judge continued. "This is what we are going to do. I will make an announcement in open court informing the jury that the U.S. government negotiated deals with these witnesses, so they would testify. The prosecution also sat with the witnesses and prepared them for trial. I assume there will be no objections." Simon and I shook our heads and indicated there were no objections. We all returned to our places in the courtroom.

The trial resumed. The judge addressed the jury and said, "Mr. Calderon and other witnesses who received immigration assistance and green cards have been given assurances the United States government would not revoke their green cards or legal statuses if they testified. Further, the government told the witnesses that they would not be deported, as long as they told the truth."

The judge turned to the witness. "Mr. Calderon, you are to answer each question honestly. If you answer the questions honestly, your green card and your legal status will not be revoked." Calderon bowed his head toward the judge as if to say yes. "Did the prosecution make any other deals with you to get you to testify today?"

"Yes, Your Honor. The attorneys said that they would help my brother obtain a visa to come here."

"Mr. Schwartz, you will honor your promise to Mr. Calderon if he tells the truth today. Do you understand?"

"Yes, Your Honor."

Now, it was my turn. I approached the witness again. "Mr. Calderon, you earlier testified that you spoke to a person on the telephone claiming to be the rabbi. Do you remember that testimony?"

"Yes."

"Was the voice of the person who claimed to be the rabbi on the telephone a younger or an older person? Was the individual a man or woman?"

"Not an old man and definitely not a woman. Maybe a younger man."

"Thank you, Mr. Calderon. No other questions."

The judge motioned to Simon, "Do you wish to follow up and ask this witness additional questions?"

"Your Honor, we have no other questions for this witness."

"The witness is dismissed. Mr. Schwartz please call your next witness," said the judge.

Luis Gonzalez, Donald McBaylor, Dorothy Wisniewski and Michael Gehrig were all individually called to testify. When one completed their testimony, the next witness was called to the stand. Each of them was a blue-collar worker who had obtained their green cards from someone claiming to be Rabbi Lefkovitz.

None of the witnesses ever met with Rabbi Lefkovitz and each testified that the voice on the phone was that of a younger person. Further, each recalled that the telephone number they called was answered by someone claiming to be an employee of the yeshiva. The operator at the yeshiva directed the caller to someone in the accounting department.

The witnesses tediously recounted their recollections to the point where the judge had to adjourn the court before each member of the jury fell asleep.

As we left court, proprietors of the newspaper stands within blocks of the courthouse, were hawking newspapers. Their headline read: "Rabbi Sells Visas and Green Cards to Illegals." The rabbi pretended that he didn't see the headlines. He ignored reporter's questions as we left the courthouse. We walked together to the train which took us to Shira who had dinner waiting for us on the table. I knew the pressure was mounting and taking a toll on her father. I contemplated how much more he would be able to take before he exploded or suffered a health condition. I questioned the soundness of his mental and physical well-being after Emah's death, knowing his weight and age.

The court recessed for three weeks to permit the observances of the Jewish New Year, Yom Kippur and Sukkot. Sadly, during this hiatus, tragedy struck at the Olympic Games in Munich, Germany. The headlines said eleven Israeli Olympians were murdered by

Palestinian terrorists.

The observance of the high holidays this year was saddened by the memory of Emah. Even the holiday of Sukkot, which is usually a joyous time, proved difficult. Shira started experiencing morning sickness during this time too. Both of us were excited by the prospects of a second child, but she was stressed because of the trial and the death of her mom. Finally, Shira met with the dean and received permission to take only two classes this semester to lessen the burden. I still don't know how she did it.

As we waited for the trial to resume, our lives adjusted to a new normal. On this Friday night, like the previous ones we waited until Rav returned from the shul. This evening however, Sara and Joel joined us for Shabbos dinner. The wives were feeding our sons while Joel and I were having a drink and nosh in the living room, waiting for his arrival to start dinner. The conversation suddenly moved from the disappointing Yankees to Joel asking me, "Can you keep a secret?"

"Of course."

"It's not official, but Sara and I are expecting."

I had to laugh. "Shira is pregnant too. Do you think they planned it?"

He laughed and said, "I wouldn't put it past them." Just then Rav came to the door and greeted us with a sad smile and the words, "Good Shabbos."

Out of respect, I permitted Rav to sit at the head of the table where I usually sat. Normally, he shared a two-minute thought from the Torah, led us in kiddush and then blessed the challah before we ate. Strangely, tonight, he elected to tell us a story that seemed irrelevant, but in time I learned its significance.

"It was the holiday of Lag B'Omer. In the Zohar, it is written that Rabbi Shim'on was arranging his affairs to depart the world on that day. The people of Meron wished to bury Rabbi Shim'on with honors in their cemetery. Warriors from Sepphoris attacked the city on a mission to deny Rabbi Shim'on a righteous burial. Just as the warriors overcame the citizens of Meron in battle, the Rabbi's corpse ignited into flames and the angels in heaven buried him up on high."

Joel, Shira and I looked puzzled, but said nothing. I remained curious. Then he lifted his wine glass, and we started the Shabbos ritual. After dinner, the rabbi retreated to his room, but not before he thanked us for everything, we had done for him, and his family. It was as if he was saying a permanent goodbye.

The following Sunday morning, I sat down with Rav to discuss what we had learned from the trial. He had kept telling me before Emah died that he wasn't quite clear about all the ongoings of the accounting office operations. After her death he hadn't wanted to discuss anything related to the trial. Now, I needed him to concentrate and provide me with answers. After listening to the immigrants' testimonies, I was fairly sure Rav would have a better idea of the accounting procedures and who conducted what duties.

"Explain to me the inner workings of how money flowed at the yeshiva and at Exodus. Who handled the money? Who made the financial decisions? Who could have pocketed the money? Who could have gone to the currency exchanges to convert the checks to cash? Never mind, answer this question first. Rav, if an envelope of money came into the yeshiva, who opened the mail?"

He thought hard and long before he spoke. "I think, if the secretary sees that an envelope contains a check, she will give it to either my son, Yehuda or the controller, Mayer."

"Who records the money into the books at the yeshiva?"

"That would be mostly David, but Yehuda or Mayer could also. Then, one of them would deposit the money in the yeshiva's bank account."

"Who wrote out the checks and recorded them when the yeshiva purchased goods and services?"

"That could be Yehuda, Mayer or David Ben Aaron. All three have access to the checkbook, but David records the payments in the computer."

"If a check comes in for deposit with your name on it, are you the only one who can endorse it or sign the back of the check?"

"They have a rubber stamp with my signature on it to endorse checks. Then they can deposit the monies in the bank. I guess they could also ask me to sign the check and then they would deposit it."

"Who has access to this rubber stamp?"

"I think there are several signature stamps. Several people have them, including the secretaries. It usually sat on their desktops."

"Who was authorized to use the signature stamp without asking your permission or without notifying you?"

"Everyone in the office was authorized to use it. If they needed my permission for every deposit or check payment, I would never have a free minute to do anything but take care of the financial paperwork of the place."

"How often are check payments brought to you for your review? Do you verify or double check if the payment is made out to the correct person or double check if the amount is correct?"

"Honestly, I never checked. I trust my son, Mayer and David, so I never double checked the correctness of their work. Honestly, I never learned accounting and hated math."

"Now the most important question. If one of them was dishonest, who would you guess it would be?"

"I have not observed an unfaithful act by any of them." I knew that was a religious individual's way of answering the question. If he had a hunch without actual proof, he would remain silent and there was nothing I could say or do to coerce him in telling me.

"Is David the only person who typically brings checks to your office requiring your signature?"

"No, all three have brought checks for my signature and sometimes others bring them to me, too."

Hours of grueling questions and answers melted the day away and Rav was exhausted. Eventually, Shira returned home, the Rav yawned and said, "Michael, I'm tired. Now that Shira has returned home with Ben, maybe you'll let me take Ben to the park before dinner. I am tired of all these questions."

Upon seeing his grandfather, Ben ran up to his 'Saba' (grandfather) to give him a big hug and a kiss. In the mornings, Ben climbed out of his bed, walked to Saba's room and hugged him.

I shrugged my shoulders. "Don't ask me if you can take him to the park. Ask Shira. She's in charge. However, it's getting dark and Central Park is too dangerous at night. I prefer if you stayed around the neighborhood."

"Michael, you're a wise man. Women are smarter than we are. They let us think that we are wiser because they let us make an occasional decision. Always be good to her and count your days together as blessings. We never know when those days will end."

"Rav, may I offer you some advice?"

"If not you, who?"

"God told us to appreciate all the days of our lives. Our lives are holy, and we must enjoy our blessings, right?"

"Michael, thank you. I have been wallowing in self-pity. I will pray to God and beg him to forgive me. I will change my ways and be more supportive in my defense."

# The Jewish holidays were over

The rumor I heard in the street was someone at the Justice Department in Washington said, "Make a deal. We have too much at stake. The Soviets are expecting results. Don't allow this Jew off scot-free. Schwartz, if you have any political ambitions, you'd better get a conviction. Otherwise, you can kiss your political aspirations goodbye."

Simon called the yeshiva's controller, Mayer, and asked to meet with him at the FBI headquarters. Agent Johns was there to serve as extra muscle. Simon began to question him "Mayer, as the controller, you must have known monies were disappearing or had been misapplied. Didn't you?"

Mayer's attorney, Yaacov Levin responded, "What are you implying?"

Simon slammed his fist on the table. "Either you become a witness, or you will become a defendant. Now tell me what you know about cash payments. Who cashed them at the currency exchanges and who ended up with the cash?"

Yaacov usually dealt with speeding and parking tickets, so he was out of his league. He didn't know enough to ask for a proffer. So, when Mayer looked to

Yaacov for advice, his response was, "I recommend you cooperate. Do whatever the government wants you to do. You have no choice."

"We wrote checks out to cash and cashed the checks when Rabbi Lefkovitz needed monies to distribute to the poor," Mayer began to explain.

Simon was not getting answers he wanted to hear. "Don't play games with me. I'm talking about the checks payable to cash which were paid to the congressman. Also, the cashier's checks that were made payable to cash and received by the yeshiva from immigrants."

"The Russians?"

"Don't try my patience! Not the Russians, the other illegal U.S. immigrants."

Shaking and scared enough to soil his pants, Mayer said, "I didn't see any checks payable to cash or checks received from illegal immigrants payable to cash. To the best of my knowledge, we received donations payable to cash all the time. Whatever monies we received as donations were deposited into the yeshiva's bank account. The only cash given to Rabbi Lefkovitz was used for the poor."

Now frustrated, Simon demanded to know, "Who opens the mail when it arrives at the yeshiva? Who retrieves the mail at the post office box?"

"The secretary opens the mail. She gives it to Yehuda or to David who then records it in the accounting ledgers before they give it to me."

"Yehuda, that's the rabbi's son, right?"

Nervously, he began stuttering. "Y-y-yes."

"Has Yehuda been spending a lot of money lately? Buying cars, furniture or jewelry? Has he been talking about vacations or investments?"

Still shaking Mayer said, "He mentioned that he wanted to go to Israel and said he might do so the next time he was in Europe. He also mentioned he was looking at buying a new car in the future."

"Who talked to the congressman? You or Yehuda?"

"Usually Yehuda, I think. Why?"

"You will testify to that at trial and at the grand jury. If you change your testimony or tell anyone you are my witness, I will have you brought up as an accessory to the crime. That's at least five years in prison. Johns, please get the court reporter to type out his statement and have him sign it."

Simon left the room and directed one of his attorneys to "Prepare a case against the son. Bundle together a presentation as if you were going in front of a grand jury. Get Joe Marcus at the district attorney's office on the line. Once you have him on the phone, let me talk to him."

Two minutes later, Joe was on the phone. "Joe, Simon here, I have a gift for you. I would like your office to press charges against Lefkovitz's son. We have prepared the case and will deliver the evidence to you along with a list of witnesses available to testify. It will be a slam dunk conviction."

"Why am I so lucky? What's in it for you?"

"I want the kid arrested next Friday afternoon a week from now, so he'll have to be detained until Monday while waiting for his bail hearing. I want him sent to the Tombs where I will have a surprise for him. Afterwards, I expect he'll testify to anything and everything I tell him."

"Why don't you want to charge him as a co-conspirator?"

"I don't want anyone to suspect that I am involved should something 'happen to him.' There are all kinds of stories that bad things happen at the Tombs."

"Simon, you are a bastard. I'm glad you're on our side. Don't worry. We'll coordinate with your people."

"Remember. Arrest him late enough in the afternoon so that he can't have a bail hearing until Monday. I'll make sure he has a gruesome experience, and he would prefer to testify against his father than return to the Tombs lock-up."

Joe Marcus arranged for the Brooklyn police department to arrest Yehuda on Friday at 4 p.m.

I didn't have a clue what was in store for Yehuda when we returned to court Friday morning. I was relaxed when Simon arrived at the courtroom inexplicably late. He placed papers at his desk and then approached the clerk of the court. Simon requested an additional one-hour delay from the clerk before the start of today's trial. Courts generally accommodate such a request when there is a chance for the parties to

201

negotiate a settlement of the case, and this court was no different.

Simon signaled me with a hand wave indicating his desire to meet in the small conference room. We entered the room together and sat face to face. "Good morning, Michael. You know we have enough evidence to send your father-in-law away for forty years. I feel for him and for you especially after the loss of his wife. The best deal that the United States attorney general has permitted me to offer is the following: guilty pleas to both money laundering and bribery of a public official. He'll get ten years but will only have to serve three."

Not so fast, I thought. I wanted Simon to question his winning hand by asking, "What do you have? I haven't seen any convincing evidence that would prompt a jury to find my client guilty beyond a reasonable doubt."

I knew this wasn't necessarily true, but I wanted to see if they had something more damning than what I hadn't seen. I was secretly worried if Rav was convicted on the campaign donations or bribery charges he could be sentenced to a ten-years in jail. Three years might be too good a deal not to accept.

"Michael, between the two of us, and I will deny that we ever had this conversation, we will be calling Boyle as a witness. He will say anything to reduce his prison term. Do you understand what I'm saying? I need an answer now from you."

I took a deep breath, bit my lip and countered,

"Simon, what if the rabbi pleads guilty and receives a ten-year suspended sentence: no jail time? Look at him; how long would he last in prison? Do you want to incarcerate a recently widowed religious old man whose only crime was to do good? Give him a thousand hours of community service and call it a day."

"Sorry, you got our best deal."

"Give me a few minutes to discuss the offer with my client." Simon agreed.

We re-entered the courtroom. Simon returned to the prosecution's table and I motioned for Rav to join me in the little conference room. We talked for fifteen minutes. I told him the score and shared the government's offered plea agreement and advised that it was good deal worth considering. In fact, I told him that his chances of being found not guilty were less than 25 percent. "It is very likely the jury will find you guilty and you could go away for more than ten years."

"Michael, I will not plead guilty to something that I did not do."

"Aba, you knowingly gave monies to a congressman, even if you didn't know it exceeded campaign contribution laws, you violated the law. You paid monies expecting the congressman to perform certain favors for you in return. They can put you away for that. All you would need do is just plead guilty. You would serve a short three years at a minimum-security facility. You would be able to work as a chaplain and serve the spiritual needs of the inmates."

"Michael, what you say is true. I did pay monies expecting certain favors. But I am not guilty. I have put my trust in God and in you. Only when I am found not guilty will my name be cleared. I am not doing this just to clear my name, the stakes are much higher than that. If I am found guilty it will be an enormous blow to the fundraising efforts to free Soviet Jews."

I sat in the court's conference room contemplating my next move. I believed Rav viewed me as God's agent sent to save him and the Soviet Jews. Last evening, Shira shared with me a Talmudic saying, "The greater the struggle, the greater the reward." I know she was expecting me to perform miracles and to be their pillar of strength. I hoped that I could live up to both of their expectations.

I walked into the courtroom, sat down at the defense table and looked toward Simon and I shook my head to indicate we had rejected the deal. Simon told the clerk there was no deal. The clerk signaled to the judge to call the court to order. The judge then asked Simon to call his next witness.

"Our next witness is Congressman John Boyle."

The heavyset Irishman was sworn in and took his place in the witness chair. He used his fingers to brush his gray hair back as he sat down. Simon began by asking Boyle the typical opening questions: Who are you? Where do you live and work? Then, Simon asked fundamental questions germane to his case.

"Mr. Boyle, would you please tell the court when

and in what context you first met Rabbi Lefkovitz."

"Sure. I met Rabbi Lefkovitz in the summer of 1968. I was campaigning for re-election before the November race and raising funds. I met with various members of the Jewish community from the four boroughs of New York. They told me that they were concerned for their Jewish brothers in the USSR. Rabbi Lefkovitz was one of the leaders with whom I met."

"I told them that I would only be able to help them with their cause if I won the November election. To achieve that goal, I needed money to pay for advertising and staff salaries. The Jewish leaders committed to support me by making generous campaign contributions, on the condition that after the election, I help Soviet Jews obtain immigration visas and support Congressman Jackson's trade bill."

"What was the financial commitment that Rabbi Lefkovitz made to you?"

"He committed to pay me three thousand dollars monthly."

"Even after the election?"

"I'm sorry. Are you asking me if he continued to pay me monies after the election?"

"Precisely."

"Yes, he paid me monies after the election." Simon let Boyle ramble on for thirty seconds before he asked Boyle for details about how the scheme worked. Boyle responded, "The rabbi came to me and sought visas for specific individuals from the USSR. A congressman starts raising money the day after an election and spends his entire two years in office raising money for his next campaign, so I was willing to oblige the rabbi. I needed the money."

"How much did the rabbi pay to you after the election?"

"Three thousand dollars every month like clockwork."

"Did you meet the rabbi in person after your initial meeting?"

"Yes, we met in person once or twice, I think. I only recently learned that one or two checks came from his Exodus fund, a not-for-profit corporation. Most of the check payments to me came from his yeshiva's bank account."

"Was it legal for a not-for-profit entity to make political donations of thirty-six thousand dollars?"

Boyle hit his fist on the edge of the witness box as he said, "No, it wasn't legal. In fact, churches and temples cannot make political donations."

Simon smiled at the jury and continued his examination of the witness. "Did you tell the defendant that the donations made to your political campaign were illegal?"

"No, because I didn't realize he was making the payments from his charity. However, I did tell him that he should consult with his attorney to understand the legal implication of political contributions before making them."

Rav sat in court reading religious texts, so I didn't think he was paying attention, until he grabbed my arm and handed a piece of paper, 'HE LIED'. Obviously, he was listening to every word. Until then, I'd had my reservations about whether he was paying attention.

"Did you meet with the defendant again to discuss other payments to you?"

"Yes."

"Tell us about that meeting."

"It was spring of 1970. The rabbi told me that he sought visas or green cards for illegal immigrants who were already in the U.S. We had a discussion and I told him that he would be required to pay me one thousand dollars for each person needing a permanent visa or green card."

"Were these visas to benefit Soviet Jews?"

"No. They benefited illegal aliens who were already here in the United States, I believe."

"What did he say after you said you wanted a thousand dollars for each visa?"

"He agreed to pay me without a question being asked." The jury looked at Rav with unveiled contempt.

"Explain to the jury what kinds of visas were being sold."

"These visas would grant each illegal immigrant permanent status to stay, live and work in the United States."

"Did you provide instructions as to the manner you were to receive these one-thousand-dollar payments?"

"I told him that I wanted checks or cashier's checks payable to cash. Initially, I had him make the checks payable to me. Then, I told him to make payable to cash so I could hide the money without paying taxes. The check payments were written from the yeshiva's bank account."

"Congressman, how would we characterize these payments to you? As illegal bribes?"

"Yes, these were illegal bribes."

"Did you plead guilty to the crime of receiving illegal bribes and income tax invasion in a federal court proceeding earlier this year?"

"Yes, I pleaded guilty to the bribes that I received from the rabbi sitting there," he said, pointing his finger at him. Then, he repeated himself. "Yes, I pleaded guilty to the crime of accepting bribes." Members of the jury shook their heads in disgust.

"Did the rabbi know that these were bribes?"

I jumped up before the witness was able to utter a syllable and said, "I object, Your Honor. There is no way the witness could have known what the defendant knew or didn't know at the time these alleged payments were made."

Simon responded, "Your Honor, let me withdraw the question and ask it another way." The judge granted Simon's request.

"Mr. Boyle, did you tell the defendant that this was an illegal transaction?"

"I did. I explained it to him and insisted that the

check payments be made payable to cash."

"How much bribe money did the rabbi pay monthly?"

"About three thousand dollars a month to my campaign fund and another three to four thousand dollars paid to me in cash bribes."

"Thank you, Mr. Boyle. Your Honor, we have concluded our direct examination of this witness."

The judge looked at me. "Your witness."

I strolled slowly to the witness box while gathering my thoughts before I asked my first question. Boyle's testimony was so damning that I feared Rav would die in prison. I stared at Boyle for a second and then began my cross-examination. "Why are you testifying today?"

"To tell the truth about transactions that occurred over the past three years."

"Isn't it true that you hope by testifying today, you hope to reduce the number of years that the court may sentence you to serve in prison? Isn't that why you are coming forth today with your testimony?"

Boyle shook his head before saying, "I was promised nothing by the prosecution."

"Thank you, but that is not what I asked. Do you hope that by testifying today you will be given a reduction in your sentence? Please don't look at Mr. Schwartz. Mr. Schwartz is not allowed to answer this one for you."

As I said, "Don't look to Mr. Schwartz," my comment was not lost on the jury as the onlookers chuckled.

"I guess, I am hoping that my participation here today will be considered at my sentencing hearing."

"I thought that every election campaign was ethically responsible for screening for foreign, corporate and not-for-profit donations. Would you say that is a true statement?"

With a slight nod of his head Boyle answered, "Yes, in theory. But with so many donations coming in, it's difficult to catch everyone. Some slip through the cracks."

"So, you and your staff didn't notice that the rabbi's not-for-profit charity paid you what you described as illegal payments for twenty-four straight months, and no one caught this?"

He shrugged his shoulders and said, "I guess not."

"Hmm. Isn't a three thousand dollars payment a rather large campaign donation?"

"It's not the largest, but it's larger than the average amount that I typically received."

"Why then did it go unnoticed?"

"I don't know."

"You said that in the spring of 1970, you met with the rabbi and discussed the cash monies for payments for illegal immigrant visas. Can you pinpoint a date or even a week when the two of you met in person?"

Boyle had begun sweating and wiping his forehead. Next, he started to squirm and began to fidget. "I think it was the first week in March."

"Are you positive you met him during the first week in March?"

"Yes, it was positively the first two weeks of March."

"Physically in what location was this meeting held?"

"I can't remember where we met. It was too long ago."

"What if I told you the rabbi was out of town at that time of the month? Could your conversation have been on a telephone?"

"I'm sorry. It could have been a telephone conversation my memory isn't what it used to be. I get confused with dates and meetings. I have so many of them."

"Hmm. Did you call the rabbi?"

"He called me. The rabbi said he had a plan for us both to make money."

"Was the call long distance?"

"I don't remember. I don't think so, why?"

Simon stood up and protested. "Your Honor, this line of questioning is irrelevant."

I retorted, "Your Honor, the rabbi was in Europe negotiating with Soviet officials during the first two weeks of March 1970. We will introduce copies of airplane tickets to verify the exact dates he was there."

I really wasn't sure of the exact dates he was in Europe. I remembered however that Rav had told me during one of our meetings that the last time he traveled to Europe was in the beginning of March 1970. I was sure Boyle was lying and I wanted him to sweat. Fortunately, Boyle got flustered and his story began to unravel as I continued subjecting him to additional questions.

"Now, Mr. Boyle, whom did you talk with during the first week of March on the telephone? Was it Rabbi Lefkovitz? Or possibly someone else?"

"Yes, I believe that I discussed the terms with one of the rabbi's underlings. Most of my dealings were with the controller or his son, I'm pretty sure."

"So, we went from a physical meeting with the rabbi to a telephone call with his underlings. What is the correct story? You've confused me."

Boyle stuttered as he wiped the sweat beading on his forehead with his handkerchief. "I talked to an unidentified person."

"Did you ever personally talk with or physically meet with the rabbi to discuss illegal immigrants or green card bribes?"

"No, sir." At this point, Boyle was wiping profuse amounts of sweat from his face with his hand as he reached for the water container and poured himself a drink. His shaky hands caused some of it to spill.

I said, "Your Honor, no further questions of this witness."

The judge asked Schwartz if he wanted to redirect his witness. Simon approached the witness. "Did the rabbi tell you that you were to deal with his subordinates after your initial agreement to provide campaign financing?"

McClain gulped down some water and said, "Yes, I was told to deal with the subordinates only."

"What did you assume when the rabbi told you to deal with his subordinates? Perhaps he wanted to shield himself from any association with an illegal business enterprises?"

I stood up. "I object, Your Honor. The prosecution is leading the witness. In addition, Mr. Schwartz is requiring the witness to speculate on the mindset of the rabbi. Finally, there has not been any evidence so far introduced in these proceedings that even suggest the rabbi had knowledge of any business relating to the selling of green cards to illegal immigrants."

Simon countered, "Your Honor, the Mafia kingpins never got their hands dirty. These gangsters delegated the illegal negotiations and illegal actions to others."

I quickly and loudly objected. "Your Honor, Mr. Simon is fixated on 'The Godfather' again. My client is not Marlon Brando. He doesn't have his looks nor his blond hair." The jury members smiled and chuckled. "The rabbi knew nothing of this illegal green card selling business. Please instruct the jury to disregard the Mafia comparisons which are meant to prejudice the jury and my client."

At this point, everyone in the court seemed attentive when I made the Brando analogy. However, Simon wasn't about to give up on his comparison. He kept associating 'The Godfather' with the rabbi. I worried that when the jury eventually deliberates, they would remember Simon's comparison to a Mafia's illegal enterprise and forget that the judge told the jury to disregard it.

The judge quickly ruled in my favor. "The jury is to ignore all statements related to the Rabbi instructing his subordinates to negotiate the sale of green cards. The jury is to also disregard any association between Rabbi Lefkovitz and the Mafia including 'The Godfather'. Mr. Schwartz, in the future, please refrain from making any comparisons to the movie, its characters and the defendant. Do you understand?"

Simon nodded his head as he said, "Yes, Your Honor."

The judge told Simon and me to approach the bench for a sidebar. "Mr. Schwartz, did you know that Mr. Boyle fabricated a portion of his testimony?" Boyle was listening as the judge spoke to Simon in a muffled tone. As the judge asked Simon the question, Judge Weinberg watched the witness's eyes and reaction. Boyle sank into the witness chair and winced.

"No, Your Honor. He misled us too." Boyle's mouth was wide open at this point. Boyle was obviously in shock when Schwartz coldly stared into the judge's eyes and lied. But Judge Weinberg was not about to be fooled. He knew that Simon was stretching the truth beyond acceptable bounds. Boyle was excused as a witness.

I looked at the jury and noticed several pairs of eyes

following me. I'm not sure if they comprehended today's interactions. Did the jurors hear my discrediting of Boyle's original testimony, or had the length of his testimony and the complexity of the interactions left the jurors in a state of confusion? Who did the jury believe? Did the jurors understand that Simon was being unethical?

"Your Honor, there was a long direct and cross-examination of the last witness. May we have a short recess?" I asked.

"The court will take a fifteen-minute recess."

The afternoon newspaper headlines read, 'Boyle lied to save his skin'.

The fifteen minutes allowed me to throw refreshing, cold water on my face. I had hoped for additional time to enjoy a Coke, but it was not to be.

The clerk announced the government's next witness. "The next witness is FBI Special Agent Mark J. Johns. Please approach the bench and swear in the witness." Johns was professionally dressed in a two-piece suit and tie. At least one of the women in the jury looked at him with a flirting eye and smile.

Simon approached Johns. "Agent Johns, how many years have you worked for the FBI and to which unit are you assigned? What are your responsibilities?"

"I have been a special agent for twelve years. I am assigned to the Financial Federal Crimes Unit covering Brooklyn and surrounding New York areas. When there is a suspected federal crime, my team investigates bank records, business transactions and conducts interviews."

"Have you investigated the yeshiva's finances including its financial transactions with Congressman Boyle including bribe monies?"

"Yes, sir."

"What, if anything, were the findings of your investigation?"

"We found the yeshiva was being used as a shield to hide an illegal business operation that provided green cards and permanent visas to illegal aliens. To facilitate this crime, bribes were paid to Congressman John Boyle."

"Who oversaw the yeshiva and their banking activities?"

"The only person permitted to sign checks without a co-signer was Rabbi Moshe Lefkovitz. The controller, the rabbi's son, Yehuda Lefkovitz and David Ben Aaron were also signatories, however any check signed by them required two signatures. Rabbi Moshe Lefkovitz was the executive head of the yeshiva."

"Was Rabbi Lefkovitz the officer of any other entities? If so, what were the names of these entities?"

"The FBI learned that Rabbi Lefkovitz is the president of a not-for-profit entity known as Exodus. He is also the chairman and trustee of a foreign trust known as Genesis."

"How was the Exodus entity funded?"

"All of Exodus's funds came from the yeshiva's checking account."

"Where did the monies from Exodus go, and to whom were they paid?"

"Some monies were converted to cash while other funds were paid to Genesis. The Genesis funds were used to pay bribes to foreign government officials or kept offshore for the rabbi's benefit. Being offshore we were unable to trace the flow of the funds."

"Did you prepare an analysis for the court regarding the monies received, deposited, cashed and paid to Congressman Boyle? If you did, please share with us your findings."

As Johns was about to speak, the prosecution began to place giant poster boards onto tripods to illustrate his testimony. It was easier for the jury to better understand financial numbers seeing pictures. Most jurors get weary-eyed when financial figures are mentioned, so graphs and illustrations make it easier for jurors to follow the testimony.

Johns continued. "From the currency exchanges we inspected, we found twelve thousand dollars being paid by illegal aliens to the rabbi. Of the twelve thousand dollars, we determined that six thousand dollars was converted into cash at local currency exchanges. We learned that another six thousand dollars was deposited into the yeshiva's bank accounts."

"Was the six thousand dollars per month cashed at the currency exchanges recorded in the books and records of the yeshiva?"

"No, they were not." As Johns spoke, the spectators

and reporters gasped and appeared stunned by Agent John's revelations. The apparent mood of the jury and the observers in the courtroom seemed to shift. The jury appeared convinced that the rabbi ran an illegal enterprise and bribed a congressman. The jury was fixated on every spoken word of Special Agent Johns.

"About how much money was paid to Rabbi Lefkovitz and his yeshiva over three years?"

Projecting his voice with his eyes trained on the jury, Johns said, "Four hundred thousand and thirty-two dollars." The mouth of every member of the jury opened. The spectators once again gasped.

"How much was paid to Congressman Boyle in an average month? And what proof do you have of these payments?"

"Over the three years, roughly two hundred and fifty-two thousand dollars was paid to Boyle. The yeshiva's financial books and records indicated that Congressman Boyle received three thousand dollars monthly that was paid to his political campaign fund. There were other payments averaging four thousand dollars a month were made payable to cash?"

"Do you know how much of these monies were actually received by Boyle?"

"Boyle testified at his trial, and the findings of our investigation confirmed that he received about seven thousand dollars per month."

"Is there a correlation between the four thousand dollars paid to Boyle and the profits reaped by the yeshiva and the rabbi every month?"

"Boyle swore under oath that he charged one thousand dollars for each political favor he granted, so four political favors would total four thousand dollars.

"The illegal immigrants paid three thousand dollars for their visas. Four visa sales would net the rabbi twelve thousand dollars."

"When you said political favors, how would the law categorize the nature of these payments to Congressman Boyle? Were these payments political bribes?"

"Yes, sir, these were illegal bribes."

"Has a federal court convicted Boyle of accepting bribes by exchanging monies for favors?"

"Yes, sir."

"Did you discover in the normal course of your investigation who cashed the checks at the currency exchanges?"

"I interviewed former and current employees of the currency exchanges located in Harlem. The currency exchange employees claimed they couldn't identify the person who presented the checks because all the religious folks look the same to them." The jury couldn't help but chuckle. "Most of the former employees stated however that the person cashing each check stated they were doing so for the head rabbi."

"Did you find evidence Rabbi Lefkovitz cashed or financially benefited from these monies? If not, why?"

"We found no monies. Cash could have been deposited in European bank accounts in Switzerland or elsewhere. The rabbi and his son Yehuda had numerous trips to Europe and Israel. Perhaps, he stashed the monies in safety deposit boxes at various banks around the country. It is nearly impossible to uncover hidden monies, until one attempts to spend it."

"Object, Your Honor, speculation."

"I'm going to overrule you, Mr. Goldman. The question asked of the witness is stated to offer reasons why they have not found money trails. The question and the answers offered are both reasonable and will be allowed to stand."

"Thank you, Special Agents Johns. Your witness." Simon relinquished the FBI agent to me for further questioning.

"Special Agent Johns, good afternoon. Do you recall meeting me before in my capacity as the attorney for Rabbi Lefkovitz?"

"Yes, sir."

"I assume you have interviewed many potential witnesses in this matter to date? How many would you estimate?"

"My partner and I have interviewed over forty individuals to date."

"How many of those forty individuals that you interviewed are prepared to testify that they physically met Rabbi Moshe Lefkovitz?"

"None."

"How many of the forty can testify as eyewitnesses under oath that the rabbi participated in the selling of illegal visa or green cards to U.S. aliens or the cashing of checks at currency exchanges?"

"None." The courtroom and the jury stirred in reaction to this revelation. The members of the jury looked at each other in disbelief. The judge rapped his gavel on the table to demand silence in the courtroom.

"I assume you have performed a gross income analysis based on the rabbi's spending habits and cash disbursements."

"Yes."

"Will you explain to the jury the purpose and methodology of this type of analysis?" The agent was biting his lip. He didn't seem pleased that I asked these last two questions.

Johns began to answer my question. His voice was slightly muffled. I interrupted him. "Excuse me, Special Agent Johns. Please speak up so everyone may hear what you are saying."

"The FBI performed a gross income analysis to determine if the income reported by the rabbi and his family corresponded to their purchases. We analyzed the spending habits of the rabbi and his family over the last two years. We also looked for any increase of assets created over the year and then compared any increase to his income and family expenditures."

"Is this an effective test to measure under-reported income? What were the findings of your analysis related to the rabbi's spending?"

"It is generally an effective test to identify under-reported income. From our results, we determined that the rabbi lived within his financial means. We didn't find proof of under-reported income." I paused, so all the agent's words could sink in with the jury.

"Lived within his means. Hmm. So, you are saying the rabbi's employment income was sufficient to pay the bills commensurate with his lifestyle?"

It was obvious that Johns wasn't thrilled at having to testify to facts that supported Rav's innocence. "Yes. His employment income was sufficient to pay his bills."

"During your interview with the rabbi at the federal building, did Rabbi Lefkovitz freely admit to you that he was aware of the three-thousand-dollar monthly payments to the Boyle campaign fund? Did he also say he didn't know anything about campaign laws?"

"Yes."

"Did the rabbi also tell you that he didn't know anything about payments made for the benefit of illegal aliens?"

"Yes."

"That's all I have for this witness, Your Honor."

"Your Honor, I have several additional questions for the witness." Simon slowly walked toward the jury box. "Special Agent Johns, does the gross income test prove that the rabbi didn't extort monies? Or does it prove he didn't spend the money?"

Johns smiled and said, "It simply proves he didn't spend the illicit monies that he may have received."

"Special Agent Johns, how common is it that a

criminal will make false statements in the hopes that he will not be prosecuted?"

"It's very common for criminals to lie to us."

"Thank you." Simon looked smug as he returned to the prosecution table but then he stopped and looked at me as I approached the witness again.

"Your Honor, one last question for the witness. Special Agent Johns, do you know for a fact that the rabbi was lying when he made his statements of innocence to you?"

"No sir." I walked back to the defense table and the judge excused the witness.

The clerk of the court announced, "Calling the government's next witness: Special Agent Murphy."

Simon asked the next witness, "Special Agent Murphy, please state your full name, the number of years you have been with the FBI and your current posting."

"My name is Thomas Murphy. I have been with the FBI for over ten years. I am assigned to the Federal Financial Crimes Unit. My specialty is surveillance."

"Did you investigate Rabbi Lefkovitz and what were your observations and findings?"

"The FBI maintained court authorized wiretaps on the rabbi's phones in both his home and offices. We found that the rabbi conducted conversations in various languages."

"What languages?"

"Russian, Hebrew, English and Yiddish."

"Is this common for criminals to speak in foreign languages to protect their criminal activities?"

"Many times, suspects will speak in code or speak in other languages to frustrate third party listeners or to hide criminal activities." I wanted to object but decided to wait to see where Simon was going with his questions.

"With whom did the rabbi speak when he had these foreign language conversations?"

"Soviet government officials, European citizens, individuals living in Israel and people living here in the United States."

"What did the rabbi discuss in his conversations?"

"From what we were able to translate, the conversations centered on financial deals exchanging favors with the Soviets and religious matters."

"You said 'from the best we were able to translate'. Why did you use this disclaimer in your testimony?"

"Because the rabbi may have been speaking in code to deceive us."

"In your surveillance and analysis of his bank accounts how many foreign travels did the rabbi undertake in the last three years?"

"The rabbi met with several individuals in Europe over the past three years. The last time he was in Europe was March 1970. He has since traveled to Israel numerous times. The rabbi has had countless meetings with foreign nationals including those born in the Soviet Union here in New York."

"Where was the rabbi born?"

"He was born in Lithuania, which is now part of the Soviet Union."

"When Rabbi Lefkovitz met with Soviets, is it possible that these individuals may have been foreign spies?"

The witness looked at the jury. "Yes, it is possible Rabbi Lefkovitz has been dealing with foreign spies."

Simon crossed the ethical red line by associating the rabbi with Soviet spies. My objection was so loud that everyone in the court heard it. Some say that it awakened the dead. "Your Honor, we stopped portraying the rabbi as Marlon Brando, now are we trying to poison the jury into believing he is a Soviet spy? There is no evidence that this is even a remote possibility."

I walked up to within three feet of the bench and poised myself between the judge and the jury. "These statements are meant to prejudice the jury. The defense will not stand for these unethical breaches of conduct by Mr. Schwartz."

Simon then spoke. "Your Honor, the United States has a history of Russian Jews who emigrated here and remained loyal to their homeland, like Julius and Ethel Rosenberg. They chose to spy for the Soviet government against the United States government and sell our government secrets for pieces of silver."

The courtroom was humming. The reporters waited for the court's response. Their pens were poised to write down on their note pads whether the rabbi was a foreign agent. Reporters were prepared to run to the payphones to call their editors with the bombshell headline of the decade: 'Rabbi is Soviet Spy'.

Judge Jack D. Weinberg remained calm, folded his hands, stared down and made a face that indicated that he was carefully choosing his next words. He bit his upper lip. His eyes were bulging, and his face became flushed red with anger as the seconds ticked away.

The judge could not contain his outrage any longer. All eyes in the court were focused on him and all ears were attuned so as not to miss the judge's words. When he spoke, it was initially in a whisper, "Mr. Murphy, I served as an officer in Korea. Did you serve in the military?"

"No, sir. I was recruited out of college to work for the FBI."

The judge continued. "I am Jewish. I learned Russian and Yiddish from my Russian mother. I have a cousin who works at the Soviet embassy. He's probably KGB and we go out for dinner every month or two. Am I a Soviet spy?"

Simon thought about interrupting but as he opened his mouth Judge Weinberg forcefully stated, "No one except Special Agent Murphy may address the bench until I have finished questioning this witness. Now, Mr. Murphy, answer my question!"

"Your Honor, I don't know. Anything is possible."

"Could be, because I am Jewish or because I speak

Russian?"

"Uh... uh... I haven't investigated you. Uh... uh... I don't know how to answer your question."

"Did you catch the rabbi passing military secrets? Or passing anything other than money to the Soviet individuals in question?"

"No."

"In your surveillance, including wiretaps, did the rabbi discuss anything other than visas with the Russians?"

"No. Your Honor."

Now the judge could be heard in the back row. "So, you have no proof that the rabbi is a spy except that he speaks Russian, and he is Jewish, correct?"

Sheepishly Murphy said, "Yes."

"I'm appalled that in my court, a United States assistant attorney and the government's witness, who happens to be a U.S. government employee, would insinuate that Jews are Soviet spies without a shred of evidence. After the McCarthy era, the government should be aware of the repercussions and hatred that false accusations of being a Soviet spy could cause. We have just completed a sad chapter in American history where lives were destroyed by insinuations of being a Soviet sympathizer."

The judge was lecturing to the court with his eyes trained on Simon. "I am deeply offended by the anti-Semitic references made by Mr. Schwartz. I am offended that a U.S. government employee would express such anti-Semitic statements. Counselors, approach the bench."

Once we reached the bench, the judge continued in a muted tone so that the jury would not overhear us. "Mr. Goldman, if you make a motion at the end of this trial, I will consider a mistrial. I may dismiss all charges with prejudice because of the government's actions. Mr. Schwartz, I will be filing a complaint with the bar association after this trial has concluded. Now return to your seats."

We returned to our seats as the judge spoke to the courtroom. "Members of the jury, I apologize for the testimony you just heard from Special Agent Murphy. You are instructed to disregard his entire testimony. The special agent's remarks had no substantive value and were prejudicial. Such hate filled statements must not be tolerated in our country." Despite the judge's admonitions, I feared that the anti-Semitic words of Murphy and Schwartz would be remembered by some jurors.

The next expert witness called by the government was FBI Special Agent Andrea Cummings. She testified that many of the checks deposited in the Exodus checking account and other checks from the yeshiva were checks written to Boyle's campaign fund and all were signed by the rabbi. The signatures were mostly made using a rubber signature stamp to which many people had access.

The government's last witness was the yeshiva's

controller, Mayer. He testified that Yehuda, David and Rav all had access to blank checks and monies received. All could have authorized payments to be paid from the yeshiva's bank accounts. On cross examination, Mayer admitted he too went to the post office box. When I suggested that in theory, he could have pocketed the money and run the scam without anyone's knowledge, Mayer paused and agreed with me. He also admitted the rabbi didn't even know where the blank checks were stored.

I believe that I effectively planted reasonable doubt with the jury suggesting that Rav wasn't the only person who had the opportunity and ability to run the scam of selling green cards. I reminded the jury when cross-examining Mayer, that the illegal immigrant witnesses, testified they talked to a younger person.

We recessed for the week and the trial resumed on the following Tuesday. Judge Weinberg addressed the parties and announced, "Gentlemen and ladies, the court will recess until Wednesday morning of next week. The court will be closed on Tuesday for Election Day."

Judge Weinberg looked weary from all the drama this trial had caused. He needed an extra day's rest and looked forward to the long weekend. I needed the time off too. I needed to be with my wife who was now twelve weeks pregnant. I needed a quiet Shabbos with my wife and my son. I needed to weigh the danger of introducing my first witness.

# The weekend

As Rav and I had walked out of the courthouse on Friday before the extended weekend, Flynn, one of New York's finest, unbeknownst to us had arrested Yehuda and delivered him to the Tombs after 4 p.m. Yehuda used his one phone call to reassure his wife that he had been arrested and hoped to be home before sunset and the start of Shabbos.

Outside, on the courthouse steps there was a 'Student Struggle for Soviet Jewry' protest rally. Five thousand people gathered to protest Soviet treatment of Jews. These activists were encouraging greater participation by Jewish institutions to support Soviet Jews' right to emigrate.

The television news coverage was not lost on Moscow or Washington. Simon knew that he was already flirting with being disbarred and wondered what else could go wrong as he desperately sought the conviction Washington demanded to save his career.

Rav and I boarded the crowded train home. Fortunately, a young man gave up his train seat to Rav because I didn't think he would have been able to stand the whole way to my place. Only upon my insistence did he accept the young man's kindness. I noticed he had physical difficulties walking up and down the subway station's stairs. He required frequent pauses to catch his breath. Due to his apparent deterioration of health, I made up my mind we would have to take cabs instead of public transportation in the future.

As we entered my building's elevator, I had one thought on my mind. I needed to kiss and hug my wife. This week had taken a toll on me. I had worked late every evening and we'd had little time to spend with each other. Shira greeted me at the door with a loving embrace before she retreated to the kitchen.

I lied and told her I was fine, but she was well aware how the long trial was having on both her father and me. Later that night in bed Shira leaned over and whispered, "Without your emotional support, I don't know what I would do. After Emah's passing and the legal problems, you and Ben have been the reasons that I awake every morning and make it through the day. I can't tell you how much I love you and need you both."

# Yehuda

The Manhattan Detention Complex, fondly known as the Tombs, was a fifteen-story maximum security building. The complex consisted of four buildings. State and municipal courts and offices for various agencies were housed there. The Tombs was located in the northern tower.

Two years earlier, conditions at the Tombs had been so bad there was a prisoner riot on the ninth floor. Mayor Lindsay was forced to broker a settlement to break the stalemate between the inmates and the city. The jail typically held more inmates than beds on a temporary basis. An unpublicized fact was that there was at least one attempted suicide a week and numerous sexual assaults daily.

Having arrested Yehuda, Flynn took him to the station for booking and processing before driving him to the Tombs for detention. Due to the lateness of the hour that Friday, it was too late to schedule a bail hearing as planned. Yehuda would have to wait until Monday before he would be able to see a judge about bail.

Yehuda was taken down the noisy, slow elevator to the basement, where a group of additional detention cells awaited him. Simon's goal was to get Yehuda to testify against his father by intimidating him and threatening him with hell.

When Yehuda telephoned his wife, Bracha, and told her of his arrest she was stunned and shocked. She later learned that he would be incarcerated until Monday's bail hearing. She became emotionally distraught and tried calling us.

Her first thought was to call me. She tried us at home; however, Shira and I were running late and weren't at home to receive the call.

Bracha was desperate to speak to us. Her love for her husband outweighed the embarrassment of calling me for help, but she had nowhere else to turn. Now, all she could do was cry and worry until after Shabbos was over.

Shira arrived home a couple of minutes before the Rav and I walked through the door. As I walked through the threshold the telephone rang. It was the office. I handled a client emergency and then we shut off the home phones, so no one else could disturb us until Sunday morning.

After a tough week I just wanted to spend a quiet Friday night with Shira and my son. Ben and Rav normally retired early permitting time for Shira and me to be alone. Shira cooked a tasty dinner on this warm, Indian summer night and there was a full moon.

After dinner, I grabbed two bottles of Orange Crush, an opener, a throw-blanket, and Shira and I went to the deck located on the roof to look out at the city lights and the star-filled sky. She didn't seem to mind when we took the elevator that night. We needed time alone.

We lay on a single lounge chair. I laid on my back, so her head could rest on my chest. I pulled the blanket over us for comfort. She closed her eyes and sighed, saying, "Even in the worst of times, we have each other."

I smiled because her words rang true. She was and still is the girl of my dreams. She reads my mind and comforts me when I'm down. She remained the passionate lover I met on that rainy night in Woodstock. As the evening grew cooler, I woke her, and we retreated downstairs to our bedroom. We prayed for the days when Rav's legal battles would end, and life could return to what used to be normal.

Meanwhile, Yehuda was housed in a twenty by fifteen foot dark, damp, suffocating cell. There were fifteen other inmates sharing the cell along with body lice, roaches and mice. The cell was consumed by the smell of urine and body odors. The inmates who weren't fortunate enough to score a cot slept on the cement floor, some without a blanket or a sheet.

Yehuda discovered that there was only one toilet, with a two-foot modesty panel about two feet off the ground. The metal toilet had no toilet seat. If one needed to sit, he was likely to do so on the rim, which was soiled by urine and feces.

It took about two minutes before the lice and roaches invaded Yehuda's clothes. His body began to itch. He stood and walked over to use the urinal just as two inmates stood and looked down at him. They wanted to see if it was true that Jews had small penises. Normally soft-mannered, Yehuda barked in his youthful tone, "Get away or I'll call the guards." With his penis protruding from his pants, one inmate pulled Yehuda backwards, twisted his body and punched him in the gut. Yehuda bent over and fell to his knees, unable to breathe. Then he fell to the ground, in a prenatal defensive position, holding his stomach, wailing.

"Jew, if you ever threaten me again, I will kill you. Do you understand me?"

Yehuda's body lay on the urine-soaked cement in too much pain to speak or move. The two inmates walked away, spewing derogatory words directed at Yehuda.

Hours later, the food cart came around and since there was nothing kosher for Yehuda, he had to settle for a roll and water with the promise that there would be kosher food tomorrow.

Later that evening, while most of the inmates were sleeping, the bad guys who earlier assaulted Yehuda approached him again. Those who witnessed the physical and sexual attack closed their eyes, held their tongues and prayed they would not meet the same fate. One held him, the other hit him. It was a long night.

Like most nights in the Tombs, inmates heard

howling and screams. Fear was ever-present in the air. When the lights dimmed, inmates knew assaults, rapes and physical abuse would follow. Even a few of the Tomb's guards indulged in sexually abusing inmates. The odor of urine-stained Yehuda's clothes and probably saved him from further physical abuse after the first attackers had their way with him.

Bracha, Yehuda's wife, called us again on Sunday morning, before she left to visit her husband. Now rested and in renewed spirits, I answered the telephone in an upbeat mood. "Good morning. Who's calling?"

I heard weeping and then her meek voice. "Michael, Yehuda was arrested Friday. They took him to the Manhattan Detention Complex."

I didn't want to scare her by telling her that this place was a hell hole. Instead, I told her I would go to see him, and she must remain at home and wait for my call. I was conflicted because I couldn't ethically represent both Yehuda and Rav. However, I needed to go there to see what I could do for him. Our idyllic weekend had come to a crashing halt.

Quietly, I said, "Shira, they arrested your brother, Yehuda. I am going to see him in jail. Don't tell your dad where I have gone." Shira began to ask questions that I couldn't and wouldn't answer. I promised her with my fingers crossed that I would tell her everything later, knowing she would never want to hear the truth.

On the ride to the jail, I questioned why the prosecutors would bring Yehuda to the Tombs instead of detaining him in a Brooklyn police station, given he was a rabbi and non-violent offender. Why would the D.A. risk his job in an election year arresting a rabbi before the Jewish Sabbath? Yehuda wasn't a dangerous criminal; I knew something was amiss.

Since it was Sunday, I was casually dressed, not in my normal attorney suit and tie. I went through security after providing proof that I was an attorney. I was patted down, and electronically scanned for weapons and drugs. Then I was told to wait in an attorney-client room for Yehuda. The room was once a cell; it had been converted to a consultation room for attorney-inmate meetings. It was rumored that the room was bugged. I assumed the rumors were true.

Yehuda was brought upstairs wearing ankle and wrist bracelets connected by chains. He smelled so bad; I couldn't get near him. He was in shock, with a vacant stare as he avoided eye contact with me. I have seen stares like that before in the eyes of convicts who have spent years in prison. Vietnam combat war vets who returned to the U.S. had that same glare.

Ratcheting down my anger, I softly asked, "Yehuda, why did they arrest you? What are the charges?"

He was emotionless as he spoke. "They told me that unless I testify against Aba, I will be convicted as an accessory to money laundering and bribing an elected official."

"Do you have any money to pay for an attorney?"

237

"No."

"I will get an attorney to represent you tomorrow. I will see what I can do to get you a change of clothes. There are legal ethical rules that forbid attorneys from representing two individuals in the same related legal matter. It is viewed as a possible conflict of interest. Therefore, I can't represent you."

"I will find someone I trust to represent you on Monday for your hearing. Yehuda, I want to reassure you, the prosecution has no evidence linking your father with any crime. The charges against you also are meritless."

I was about to leave when I remembered that I kept a set of gym clothes in the car. "Yehuda, I have clean gym shorts, socks, underwear, and a tee-shirt in my trunk. I'll grab them and get them to you somehow. I'll see what I can do about getting you a hot shower."

For the first time since my arrival, Yehuda displayed some emotions. He sat in the chair; his elbows rested on the table with his head in his hands. Tears outpaced the sweat dripping down his face. He raised his head and pleaded with me, "Michael, don't leave me. Please don't leave me here!"

I tried to reassure him that tonight will be better than the previous ones. "By morning," I told him, "You will be released and returned home." This place was a hell hole. Not even the attorneys wanted to visit their clients here. "Yehuda, if they come to you and demand you sign anything, do not sign it! DON'T sign anything without your attorney. Do you understand? Don't sign your name to anything." He nodded.

"Michael, I don't know if I can survive another night. They beat me up and forced me to take a man's penis in my mouth." I shivered at the thought of the brutality he had suffered. My heart ached when I thought of this rabbi and former yeshiva student who had never hurt a fly suffering in such a heinous manner. Yet, I had to keep him positive and hopeful, because I worried that suicide might be on his mind.

"Yehuda," I repeated, "Tonight will be better. I promise. Once you have a hot shower, and clean clothes, you will feel like a new person. Ask the guards to burn your bug infested clothes." With that empty promise, I left the room, the guards returned him to his cell, and I asked for Captain Clarke. I hoped he was there on a Sunday and he'd meet with me.

The guard asked if the captain was expecting me. I lied and told him that we were old friends. Every year around Christmas and Thanksgiving, most of the criminal defense legal bar association members brought food gifts to the heads of the prison, the guards and to clerks of the various courts. I gave Clarke a turkey or ham every year. These state employees can make life easier for our clients if they like you, and hell if they don't, that was the reason I gave them all holiday gifts.

He arrived several minutes later decked out in his polished shoes and neatly pressed uniform. He had a slight beer belly that covered his belt buckle. "Captain

Clarke, I hope you remember me. My name is Michael Goldman."

He yawned twice before the first words came out of his mouth. He said, "Yeah, I remember you. What can I do for you today?"

"My brother-in-law is locked up in your facility. I was hoping that if I dropped off clean clothes, he could get a shower and an accommodation where he will be safe from attacks. The last two evenings, he was sexually abused by the prisoners."

His hand opened as he said, "I don't run a country club and I can't do special favors for every criminal attorney with family members here. However, you are a lucky man. Today, we are collecting money for the employee welfare fund. Do you want to make a charitable contribution?"

I pulled out my wallet and grabbed two twenties and one ten, leaving enough money to pay for my parking. I handed him the cash and with a slight smile said, "Captain, I would appreciate any consideration you would afford my brother-in-law. By the way, I understand that this donation is voluntary, correct?"

"Of course. We don't accept bribes here in my facility. I'll see what I can do." He stuffed the money into the front right pocket of his trousers as he walked away. He was true to his word; Yehuda slept in a bed in a two-man cell after being permitted to take a shower that evening.

Arriving home, I dared not tell Shira or her father

about Yehuda's physical or mental condition. I told them that he looked okay, and I would arrange for his release first thing the following morning. They were relieved to hear that Yehuda was safe. I went into my bedroom and called Sam Smith at home. Sam was my friend formerly in the D. A.'s office. Sam had left the D.A.'s office a few months ago to hang out his shingle as a sole practitioner criminal defense attorney.

"Sam, its Michael. How is it going in your new practice?"

"Michael, good to hear from you and thanks for the plant. You should come by and see my office."

"How's business?"

"There are plenty of criminals in this city. So far, I am finding plenty of bad guys with little or no money to pay me." We both chuckled.

"Sam, I have a favor to ask and an offer for you. Since I started this federal trial representing my father-in-law, there has been so much media attention I have been offered more criminal cases than I can handle. My staff is working sixty hours a week. I have a brother-in-law who was arrested and imprisoned at the Tombs over the weekend."

"I have a conflict so, would you represent my brother-in-law, Yehuda, at his bail hearing tomorrow morning and be his defense attorney until this matter is resolved? I would be eternally grateful. The state arrested him, but I sense that Simon Schwartz has orchestrated it, so he'd be abused in jail."

241

Sam asked, "In return for the favor, what are you offering me, a good dinner?"

"After my brother-in-law's trial is over, would you consider joining my law firm?"

There was deafening silence. I thought we had been disconnected. "Michael, are you sure? I would love to be part of your firm and have a steady paycheck."

"Sam, as you already know, I started to build a boutique criminal defense law firm. You were one of the best criminal prosecuting attorneys in the state. I believe that you will be a great defense attorney, and an asset to my firm. Otherwise, I wouldn't be making the offer." Sam thanked me. I continued. "Tomorrow, plead with the prosecutor and judge to allow Yehuda to get off on his own recognizance. He has no priors and no money. He's a religious rabbi and good family man."

"I'm yours, Michael. Thank you again. I'll do my best tomorrow."

My next call was to Yehuda's wife. "Bracha, I just left Yehuda. I'm not going to lie to you. He had a terrible experience in the jail. When you come to court tomorrow, please bring a complete change of clothes including socks and shoes. My friend Sam Smith is an excellent attorney and will represent Yehuda in court. Sam will be waiting for you. I will call you later to tell you where Sam will be and what time to meet him. Yehuda will feel better tomorrow after a good night's rest. You should stay home today and not visit him."

Before I hung up, I added, "Yehuda may have

contracted lice. You may want to purchase special shampoo to rid him of it. He must also shave his beard off. Have patience and don't force Yehuda talk about his jail experiences. When he's ready, he will tell you everything." I knew that I scared her, but she was fortunate I didn't tell her the extent of his experiences.

The two days of physical abuse and horrors of the Tombs would mean that Yehuda required years of therapy before nightmares ceased to haunt him. Shira asked me what happened to Yehuda, but I could never bring myself to graphically tell her. In 1974, the atrocities at the Tombs were exposed in the New York Times. Shira read those articles and never mentioned the subject again.

Sam was quick to spot the religious young woman, wearing a wig, and long dress standing with a man's change of clothes over her arm. In fact, there weren't any other religious women in the holding tank's family room. Sam knew from my description that her name was Bracha. "Mrs. Lefkovitz?"

"Yes, how did you know?"

Sam ignored answering her question. "Mrs. Lefkovitz, I am a friend of Michael. I am here to represent your husband Yehuda today in court. Your husband went through a painful ordeal over the last few days. You may not want to press him for details. Please hand me the clothes and I will make sure that they are delivered to him."

Bracha looked at Sam with bewilderment, not

knowing how to respond. She handed him the clothes without uttering a word.

Fortunately, the day went well for Yehuda. Sam obtained his release, but not before one of the assistant district attorneys tried to intimidate Yehuda into signing a confession. At the bail hearing, the assistant district attorney asked for a million-dollar bond. The government's attorney argued that Yehuda was a flight risk. Sam took on the assistant district attorney head-to-head and won that court-battle.

"Your Honor, Rabbi Yehuda Lefkovitz has suffered enough during his detention in the Tombs. My client didn't enter the Tombs with a swollen black eye, facial bruises and fractured ribs, all of which need medical attention. As for a million-dollar bail requested by the state, the government knows that my client has no money. He lives on a weekly paycheck to put food on his table."

The judge nodded and Sam continued. "My client is no flight risk. His family and his job are in Brooklyn. I suspect the government is using him as a pawn to force this rabbi to sign a false confession and in doing so to testify against his father. Is it the government's desire to punish this rabbi with continued acts of brutality until he signs a false confession? Otherwise there no reason for the state to request bail from someone with no priors let alone arrest him and place him in the Tombs over his Sabbath."

Judge Friedman of the criminal division of the New

York's Supreme Court ordered Rabbi Yehuda Lefkovitz released on his own recognizance. However, Yehuda had to surrender his passport and agree to remain in the state of New York unless he was granted a court order permitting him to travel elsewhere. The judge then stared down the assistant district attorney. "Counselor, I want to know why this frail rabbi was subjected to brutality and abuse in your custody. I expect an answer by Wednesday. Do you understand me? I may hold you personally responsible for his condition." The judge pointed his index finger at the attorney as he uttered his words.

Sam delivered Yehuda to his wife. After he was released from custody, Bracha didn't recognize him at first. Before he and Sam parted ways, Sam told Yehuda, "Michael told me to tell you, throw the clothes he lent you in the garbage." As he pointed to the trash can, he said, "I hope you understand with a lice epidemic at the jail, he doesn't want to take any chances bringing it home."

Bracha took Yehuda to Mount Sinai hospital where they bandaged his two fractured ribs and applied ice to his swollen face. Yehuda and Bracha agreed to meet with Sam in his office the next morning to review the state's case.

Sam called me with an update. He told me that he requested from the assistant district attorney a 'bill of particulars'. It's a formal report given by the prosecution to the defendant which provides a detailed explanation of the charges brought against a defendant.

I thanked Sam. Later, I stopped by Yehuda's place with dinner for his family. Shira had arrived there earlier that morning to care for Yehuda's younger children. She also prepared the school-aged kids a snack when they returned home from school.

The acts of kindness by us and other family members were much appreciated. Yehuda eventually did recover however, he never told Bracha or another living soul what he experienced at the Tombs.

# Taking care of other matters

I had a couple of days off before the resumption of the trial. I scheduled client meetings and worked on other legal matters. Rachel Smith, formerly Levin before she changed her name to protect her parents, was a high-priced escort representing well-to-do affluent clientele. Rachel was strikingly beautiful. Originally a brunette, she now passed herself off as a natural blonde. Rachel had received threats from a former client and came to my office Tuesday afternoon to discuss her concerns and seek redress if possible.

As Pat was about to leave for the day, Rachel arrived for her appointment. Pat showed her into my office, but not before making a facial expression. Pat knew what line of work Rachel did.

After Rachel gave me a platonic hug and a kiss on the cheek, she said, "Michael, after receiving threats from a former client, I suspected being followed. Last night, I was with a client at the Park Hyatt. The police knocked on the hotel door and demanded entry. They claimed they received complaints of loud disturbance, and they were sent to investigate. They started to arrest me on suspicion of solicitation but abandoned their plans when it came to light that my client and bed partner was a high-ranking member of the police oversight commission. Michael, I'm worried. I think that Simon Schwartz is targeting me! He wants to punish me."

I put my index finger against my lips to indicate, "Don't say another word." Then I wrote a note and handed it to her. It said, 'We can't talk here in my office. It may be bugged. I want to invite you for dinner at my home tonight. This is the only way we can have a confidential conversation." She agreed by nodding her head.

She wrote back, 'Need to call someone to reschedule his appointment. Can I use the phone by the receptionist's desk?' I nodded to her that it was okay to use the telephone.

I telephoned Shira. She was not pleased when I asked if a client could join us for dinner. She reluctantly agreed. From the moment Rachel and I arrived, Shira was as cold as ice. I knew that Ben and Aba were having dinner at Ava's, Shira's sister's place, so we would be alone and could talk freely.

I made the introductions as Rachel walked into our home. Rachel was a five-foot, six-inch tall woman and wore a bright yellow summer dress with a brilliant blue sapphire pendant and matching blue sapphire dangling earrings. The three-inch ankle strap heels enhanced the look of her sexy legs. Rachel's deep blue manicure and pedicure were a perfect match for her dress. She looked like a model out of 'Glamour' magazine. Shira's radar was finely tuned, and she saw through the clothes and knew Rachel was a lady of the night.

Shira beelined to the safety of our kitchen as I offered Rachel some red wine. We had stood for a minute sharing idle chatter when Rachel motioned to me that she was going to talk to Shira.

Rachel walked over to the kitchen and asked if she could help Shira with the food preparation. Shira replied with a frosty, "No!"

So, Rachel calmly asked if they could talk, just the two of them. Rachel observed the apprehension in Shira's body language. In her profession, Rachel was keenly aware of how to read people and defuse their uneasiness.

"Shira, you have a beautiful home." Shira simply smiled. "Michael told me that you are attending CUNY. I graduated from there, with a Bachelor of Arts in English Literature." Surprised, Shira looked at Rachel and didn't ask the obvious question on her mind.

Addressing the elephant in the room, Rachel went on. "You probably want to know why I do what I do for a living."

"I would never ask. It is none of my business." Shira responded politely.

"There were very few jobs available when I graduated. The economy was bad. As a Jewish girl from the Bronx, my parents wanted to marry me off to the first doctor to be a stay-at-home mom. I didn't want that. I wanted more excitement than a hot stove."

"One day, by chance, a girlfriend confessed that she was marrying one of her clients and was retiring. She lived in a beautiful high-rise and appeared successful. She told me that she was a professional escort. I blushed when she told me the services she provided. Actually, I was shocked."

After a sip of wine, Rachel continued. "My friend offered to sell me her book of business. At first, I said no. But the more we talked, the more I became enticed by her offer. She told me that her clients took her on expensive vacations, she stayed in fancy hotels and was given luxurious gifts. Most of her clients were famous, rich and influential people.

"For many of her clients, these men simply wanted a sexy woman on their arms at a dinner party or an event. They desired a woman who was attractive and would be able to maintain an intellectual conversation. Most of the time we discuss their family, work and problems. They want a shoulder to cry on."

Shira appeared to be interested, so Rachel continued. "When I started, I was nervous. It showed. So, my girlfriend introduced me to a couple of her clients who knew that I was a beginner. These two clients mentored me, taught me to relax and gave me the self-confidence I needed So here I am today." Later Shira would tell me that could never understand how a woman could allow herself to be used for monetary gain.

Shira responded. "I don't think that I would like

that lifestyle."

"At times, I wish I had what you have, a loving family. I can't even tell my family what I do. They think that I am an advertising exec who works as an independent contractor. Someday, I hope to retire and have a traditional life." Rachel seemed sad as she shared. "The glamour has turned into a chore. I have enjoyed money but regret having to hide from people I know at a restaurant when I'm with a client. I can't maintain girlfriends because of my hours and my life can be very lonely. I can't even tell my parents what I do for work."

Abruptly, Rachel changed the topic as her eyes misted. "Tell me, what do you study at CUNY? What classes are you taking?" This was a subject that Shira was more comfortable with. The ice was broken.

After dinner, Rachel and I sat in the living room while Shira was cleaning up in the kitchen. Suddenly, we heard a loud banging on the condo door. It scared all of us. "New York police. Open up! We received complaints."

I opened the door and took an aggressive, but polite, tone with the intruders. The officers peered in and saw a normal family setting. "Officers, there were no complaints. Why have you been harassing my client? Please give me your names and badge numbers, I will be reporting both of you to Internal Affairs." The officers looked dumbfounded. They gave me their information and apologized for the disturbance, claiming that the dispatcher made the mistake.

"You see?" Rachel said, as the door closed. Shira was giving me an evil eye from the kitchen.

"Rachel, that is why I invited you here this evening. You're not the only person being harassed by Simon Schwartz. Shira's father and brother have been harassed by him, too."

Shira quick-stepped over to us to participate in the conversation upon hearing her father being mentioned. Her curiosity was piqued. I cautioned Shira. "Shira, you can never repeat what you hear tonight. You don't have the attorney-client privilege that I have, understand?" She nodded her head.

"Rachel, as an officer of the court, I cannot be involved with any unethical acts like setting up a federal prosecutor, understand?" She winked as I made my disclaimer knowing I would help her. I looked at Rachel. "So, do you have any ideas?"

"Michael, I know, but have never used, an individual who takes pictures of johns having sex. After he takes his embarrassing photographs, he contacts the johns and offers to destroy the evidence of their indiscretions for money." Shira's eyes opened wide. I don't think she knew that these types of people existed. I knew where Rachel was headed, and I liked the idea.

"Don't tell me his name, he may be a client," I said. Rachel smiled, and Shira stared at me in disbelief.

Rachel continued, "I can arrange for this event to coincide with the end of Shira's father's trial, whenever that is."

I replied, "In about ten days."

With a wicked smile Rachel said, "Yes, that would be perfect timing. I will set up a date with Simon where I'll have him meet me at a hotel room where this guy will record the goings-on. I will have him edit the pictures and videos to exclude my face before we make them public. Michael, do you have contacts or a means to leak the pictures to the press?"

"I have contacts at the Daily News and the Enquirer. Again, I cannot be associated with any of this. Understand? The best I can do is anonymously drop them on certain individuals' desks."

I looked at Rachel and said, "The pictures must be salacious and embarrassing before the press will print them. They must be something more than just sex to destroy his career."

"Michael, do you know that I fired him as a client because he is a creep and got physical with me?" Shira's eyes widened as Rachel confessed this.

"Rachel, I don't want you to put yourself in danger. Forget about the plan. It isn't worth the risk. I would like to keep you out of harm's way. There must be another way."

"I've got a better idea. I will call him as I originally suggested, however, I will tell him that I want to make up and offer him a peace offering. I'm sure he will find my gift more than acceptable."

I was confused and asked, "What? I'm lost."

"I know two women who work in tandem; they will entertain him." She giggled and continued saying, "They are into alternative sex like S and M." I knew Shira was clueless and had never heard of the term. "I'll tell him that it will take a week or two for me to arrange his gift."

Michael, do you think pictures of Schwartz whipping naked women handcuffed to the bedposts is something that would sell newspapers?"

"That should sell papers. The press will have a field-day, Schwartz's pictures will be on the front-page."

I got a dirty look from Shira before I continued, "Rachel, I like this idea. As soon as you get me the pictures, I will have them delivered discreetly to my contacts." The evening ended and Rachel left the building, taking a cab to her next appointment.

Shira and I sat in the living room waiting for Ben and her father to arrive home at which point Shira commented, "I liked her as a person. In the kitchen, I learned that Rachel is an avid reader and we read some of the same authors. This may sound terrible, but please, don't bring her back to our home."

"I won't, dear. I completely understand."

That night in bed, Shira looked at me and said, "Michael, I know Simon is a despicable individual. I am worried that we will be performing an unethical act by destroying his career. We are committing a sin through this act of revenge?"

"Shira, all we are doing is allowing Schwartz to use his God given free will. He will decide if he wants to partake in what Rachel is offering. No one is forcing him."

"I guess that's why you are a good lawyer. Everything sounds reasonable and acceptable."

"I'm sorry for bringing Rachel into our home tonight. I hoped to meet with her in private but didn't want Simon to learn that I participated in the plan just in case it backfires. You are the only woman I have ever loved, and I know that our home is sacred. I will not violate this trust again." She thanked me and held me.

# The defense starts

Simon had hoped to extract a confession from Yehuda and call him as his final witness. Without Yehuda, the government reluctantly concluded their case.

I spent the weekend before the next court hearing debating if I should call Rav as a witness. If I put him on the stand, would the jury find him to be a brilliant, goodhearted, religious man? Or would they see him as a depressed individual unworthy of sympathy? Would he be able to tell his story in a manner where the jury perceived him as a hero? Or would words dribble from his mouth and he would appear guilty?

How would the rabbi hold up to Simon's intense cross-examination of him? Would he lose his temper, or remain calm? These questions haunted me as I weighed the cost benefit of Rav testifying.

Constitutionally, a defendant is not required to testify in his or her own behalf. In our system of justice, it is the duty of the prosecution to prove guilt, not the defendant to prove his innocence. With that being said, I have learned that the prosecution will infer guilt if the defendant does not take the stand. At times, the jury will assume the defendant is guilty if he or she fails to confront their accusers on the stand to proclaim their innocence.

I shared my dilemma with Shira and asked, "I'm worried if I should call your father as a witness. I don't know if he will come across as the good man he is, or will the jury view him as a depressed and guilty man?" "Michael, go to him. Talk to Aba. Make him understand your concerns and let him decide. If he wants to clear his name, he must put forth the effort." Once again, my wife gave me good advice.

I was worried that Rav could be found guilty on some charges of bribery and campaign financing violations. The case was not that cut and dry, and I couldn't predict the jury's mindset.

Last week, I had filed a 'motion for a directed verdict.' If the court ruled in my favor, the defense could rest, and the case would be dismissed with prejudice, and Rav would be found not guilty.

These motions are rarely granted by judges because the court prefers to let the legal system run its course allowing the jury to determine the fate of the defendant.

If the judge denies my direct verdict motion, I can file a 'N.O.V.', (notwithstanding the verdict) motion. In this motion the defense appeals the jury's verdict to the judge, saying the jury got it wrong. In other words, please rule for the defendant regardless of the jury's decision. I would keep that motion in my back pocket, just in case.

If the jury rules against Rav I could still make a motion for a mistrial because of Simon's unethical courtroom abuses. We had options, depending upon the outcome of the jury's decision.

I poured Rav a glass of Scotch straight up and we discussed my concerns. He stroked his beard twice, nodded his head and said, "I must tell my story. Our cause is too important. Lives depend on the outcome of this trial."

"Rav this will not be a cake-walk, Simon will throw questions and accusations quickly at you. You must allow me the time to prepare you for the questions and answers." I hoped that I was doing the right thing by letting him go on the stand. Time would tell.

I started to prepare him for trial. I wanted him ready to answer the questions, so I treated it as a dressed rehearsal and badgered him like Schwartz would do to see his reaction. I instructed him how to answer the question pressing the point that his delivery was just as important as the words. I instructed him in body language and how to make eye contact with the jurors. I said, "Talk directly to the jury, not me or Schwartz. It's important you connect with them." After rehearsing late into the morning, he was prepared.

It was a gray, gloomy Wednesday morning following Tuesday's Richard M. Nixon's re-election victory. Nixon won by the widest of margins ever in history over his Democratic opponent. We were now in the courtroom. The first item on Judge Weinberg's docket were for the judge to rule on last week's pending motions.

Judge Weinberg said, "As for the defense's motion for a directed verdict to dismiss, while the direct evidence against the defendant is limited, there is sufficient circumstantial evidence for this matter to proceed. I will permit the jury to weigh the facts of this case and deny the defense's motion." I was disappointed, but not surprised.

The jury was now ushered into the courtroom and the judge asked, "Mr. Goldman, are you ready to call your first witness?"

"Yes, Your Honor. The defense will call Rabbi Moshe Lefkovitz as our first witness."

Rav proudly stood up, pulled his shoulders back and walked proudly to the witness chair bearing the stature of a dignified, proud man. He wore a neatly pressed black suit, white shirt, shined black shoes, black tie and sported a black fedora. He removed his hat when he lifted his right hand, promising to tell the truth. The clerk of the court administered the modified swearing-in oath given to religious individuals.

I began by asking, "Please state your full name and your profession."

Rav looked straight at the jury, making eye contact with each of them as he proudly said, "I am Rabbi Moshe Lefkovitz. I am the sixth generation of rabbis who were scholars in both the Talmud and the Zohar."

"Where do you reside?"

"I live in your spare bedroom on a sofa bed." The court laughed. The humorous response eased the tension in the courtroom. Even the judge chuckled.

"Are you currently employed? If not, where were you last employed?"

"I am currently unemployed. I was employed at the Bol Shuva Yeshiva in Flatbush. The yeshiva terminated my employment contract when this legal action against me was published in the newspapers."

"When employed at the yeshiva, you were paid a considerable amount of money as a consultant and an advisor. Who paid you these monies? Why did these people pay you?"

"I am a student of the Zohar otherwise known as the art of Jewish mysticism. People consider me a mystic. Individuals believe that I have deep insight into life and into the world to come. So, men and women, old and young, from all walks of life seek my opinions and advice and pay me for my pearls of wisdom."

"How much consulting income did you earn while working annually? What happened to these monies?"

"I earned hundreds of thousands of dollars every year. All the money I raised were deposited into yeshiva's bank accounts. The monies were used to pay its bills, to support Jews in the Soviet Union who are being oppressed and support the yeshiva's educational mission." This testimony was eye-opening to the jurors.

"In your employment contract I have now given you and a copy of which is marked as defense's exhibit number, one hundred and twenty, does it state that you are required to donate all your earned consulting income back to the yeshiva?"

Rav's index finger pointed to the paragraph as he read it out loud. "No! The employment contract states, here in section nine, that I am entitled to keep all earned consulting income. The yeshiva has no claim to these monies."

"Who was entitled to keep this consulting income?" "I earned it; it belonged to me. If I wanted to keep it, I could have kept the money. If I did, I would be a financially wealthy man today."

"You just testified that you allowed the various charitable organizations to retain the monies you earned. Why?"

"I am a wealthy man." With that statement, all eyes in the courtroom were trained on the rabbi as they waited for him to continue with his testimony. "I have my children, grandchildren, and God has been good to me. I was fortunate to have my wife of blessed memory for over forty years."

Rav paused for several seconds as he wiped his eyes. "In my opinion, there is only one purpose for having money, and that is to perform good deeds by helping others. And that's what I did with the money, I helped the poor, saved lived and educated the young." Simon and I both took notice that the jury smiled warmly as he testified.

"So, all the money that you earned consulting was retained by yeshiva, your shul, provided for the needy and save Jewish lives in the Soviet Union?"

"Yes."

"What was your motive in helping Soviet Jews?"

"Approximately five years ago, I participated in a fact-finding mission with several Jewish organizational leaders to Russia. We heard stories that the Soviet government was punishing their Jewish citizens because Israel won the 1967 Six-Day War. My parents spoke Russian in the house and Yiddish, whenever they wanted to keep secrets from me and my siblings. Eventually, I became fluent in both languages."

"In Russia, I met with refuseniks. They told me, in their mother tongue, about the financial and physical abuse they endured simply because they applied for exit visas. They wanted to travel to Israel. Instead, the Soviets beat them, fired them from their jobs or worse.

"I remember listening to one man whose wife and children left him, and his family disowned him. He lost his job because he wanted to practice his faith. I swore to him and to God on that day that I would devote my last breath helping him and people like him in their quest for freedom."

"So, what did you do when you returned from that trip?"

"I joined a task force of Jewish community leaders who sought assistance from congressmen and senators to apply pressure on the Soviets to free our Jewish brethren. I was told that Soviet government officials regularly go to Western Europe. One of the former refuseniks I knew helped arrange meetings with key individuals who had oversight on the issuance of exit visas. With his assistance, we bribed the Soviet officials to issue visas."

"Was the payment of these monies legal?"

"I believe that my actions are legal. In the Talmud, one is required to pay the ransom to free the captives. Here we paid the Soviets to gain the freedom of the oppressed."

"I understand why you paid money to the Soviet officials, but why did you pay money to Congressman Boyle?"

"A group of Jewish community leaders made a deal with Congressman Boyle. If we donated money to his political campaign, he would help us obtain visas for the Jews who chose not to go to Israel. They needed to go somewhere, and the Jewish communities here agreed to adopt these individuals and their families and to provide for their financial and social needs."

"How much did you agree to pay the congressman?"

"On behalf of the yeshiva, I made a commitment of three thousand dollars per month."

"Did you pay him any other monies in addition to the three thousand dollars to Congressman Boyle's campaign fund?"

Rav looked directly at the jury and then he looked at Simon and forcefully said, "No!"

"Before being charged with a crime, were you ever made aware of a business operating in the yeshiva where visas and green cards were sold to illegal immigrants?"

Even louder, he said, "NO!"

"Did you receive cash monies from the yeshiva?"

"Yes. I regularly received cash monies that I used to disburse to the poor and the needy. These people lived mostly in my neighborhood and they needed the funds to put food on their table, schooling for a child or to pay a doctor's bill." Again, the jury responded warmly by smiling at hearing his answer.

"Regarding the monies you paid to Boyle, did you know you were violating campaign finance laws? Did you seek the advice of anyone concerning campaign finance laws?"

"No! No one told me that there were campaign laws limiting my contributions or the types of donations the yeshiva could make. I thought, because Boyle approached me, as the figurehead of a not-for-profit organization, that it was legal to make campaign donations. If I knew these contributions were illegal, I wouldn't have had the not-for-profit entity pay any monies to his campaign committee."

I continued to ask softball questions. I wanted the jury to view the rabbi as a believable and likeable individual. For two hours I asked him questions and he answered them in his own humble words, detailing his accomplishments, his international charitable work and how he negotiated with the Soviets.

The court took a brief recess. When the trial

resumed, I asked Rav to explain the purpose of his charitable work and why he formed the Exodus organization and the Genesis Trust. He explained to the jury, "All the monies I received were accounted for by independent third-party employees of the yeshiva and annually audited and verified by a certified public accountant firm."

"Rabbi, did you concoct a financial scheme to steal monies?"

"NO! Michael, I am a simple man. I know religious books and laws. I know nothing about accounting. When my wife of blessed memory was here, she maintained the household finances because I couldn't. I handed her my paycheck, and she would give me an allowance. If I spent the money that she gave me, I knew that she wouldn't give me anymore." There were numerous chuckles from the courtroom.

"Rabbi, couldn't you have just grabbed a check from the yeshiva or ordered someone to forge your name on it and run to the currency exchange and bring you back a big, fat wad of cash?"

"I have no knowledge of the accounting of the monies. Never did I tell anyone to cash checks for me or to give me cash other than the cash that was given to the poor. Never did I ever tell someone to do anything improper. I wouldn't know how to do the bookkeeping. As a matter of fact, I don't even know where the accounting employees keep the financial books, or the yeshiva's checks."

"And how do we know you didn't sign checks for your own benefit?" I queried.

"I signed whatever checks the yeshiva employees gave to me to sign without inspecting them. It is possible I signed checks I shouldn't have, but not knowingly."

My final question was, "Have you ever stolen anything since you have become a rabbi?"

That question shocked the entire courtroom. They asked themselves, why would I ever ask such a damaging question? There was quietness as everyone wanted to hear the answer.

There was a pregnant pause before Rav spoke. "I have stolen very few things in my life. I have stolen other people's good ideas and I have stolen quotes for a sermon. As a rabbi, I prefer to say I borrowed them." The jury chuckled. "However, I have always given the other person credit for their words or ideas." Even the judge smiled.

By early afternoon, I had completed my direct examination of the rabbi. Judge Weinberg ordered the court to recess for an hour and a half lunch break. Before excusing the jury, the judge said, "Mr. Schwartz, when court resumes, you may begin your cross-examination of the witness."

After lunch, the rabbi was prepared for Schwartz's questions. Simon started his cross examination at a deliberately slow pace. He looked at Rav, smiled and pretended to be a likable person. He proceeded to ask a series of thoughtful but hypothetical questions. "Rabbi Lefkovitz, when you have a question in Jewish law, what do you do?"

The rabbi looked at Simon. He paused as he contemplated his response, suspecting, rightly so, that the question was a trap. "If I don't know the answer, I would ask another scholar."

"If they don't know the answer, do you research the question until you find a satisfactory answer?"

"Yes."

"So, Rabbi, if a congregant of yours approached you and asked whether a certain type of food was kosher or not, would you research it?"

"Yes." He seemed hesitant with his answer, trying to make sense of where the question was going.

"Would you advise others to research questions in Jewish law before performing an act or eating a food that may be religiously forbidden?" I jumped up before Rav could respond.

"I object, Your Honor. This whole line of questioning of the witness is not relevant to the matter at hand. The questions require theoretical answers and have no bearing on the facts in this case."

Simon retorted, "Your Honor, I believe my questions go to the issue of whether the rabbi intentionally ignored the law because it suited him to do so. I want to know if he knew he had a duty to research the law before paying charitable funds from his not-for-profit entities to Congressman Boyle and the Soviet agents."

"Overruled. Mr. Schwartz, you may continue, however, if your line of questioning fails to bear fruit, I will cut you off." I wanted to further protest but decided not to anger the judge. I would wait until the redirect to clarify any questionable answers.

The judge looked at the witness and said, "Rabbi Lefkovitz, you may answer the question."

"I would generally tell someone they should obey the Jewish laws on a particular issue and if they didn't know the answer, they should ask their rabbi. However, a Jew is commanded to disobey the laws of God to save a life. There is no law greater duty than saving a life. The Torah and the Talmud tell us this. I saved lives with the money I paid out."

"So, would I be correct in saying you would have knowingly violated campaign laws if you thought you were saving a life?"

I repeated my objection, but the judge overruled my objection and ordered the witness to answer the question.

"Yes, Mr. Schwartz, I would violate a law to save a life. Regardless if it was a man-made law or if it was God's law."

"Rabbi Lefkovitz, were these Jews in the Soviet Union going to be immediately killed if you didn't pay the bribes? If so, when?"

"I don't know if they were threatened with immediate physical death, but their souls were being destroyed. Death can be more than physically inflicted. Destroying the soul is akin to death."

Simon tried his best to tie Rav to the illegal immigrant bribes, suggesting the rabbi was the boss and should have supervised the goings on at the yeshiva. He even tried to get Rav to speculate as to who might have been guilty of running the bribery scam.

When Simon suggested, "Your son, Yehuda, had both the motive and means to commit these crimes, didn't he?" Simon hoped by uttering the son's name, would unleash Rav's rath and desire for revenge.

For the first time during his testimony Rav appeared emotional. His face reflected the anger in his heart, and I worried what he would say. "My son Yehuda is a scholar with a good soul who performs good deeds to benefit others. He would not steal. He would not say a bad word against another person. My son values learning above money. Anyone who does harm to a person like my son will have hell to pay in this or the world to come."

Simon completed his cross-examination; he was less confident now that there would be a conviction. He knew his case was being undermined by the rabbi's powerful testimony.

I could have asked Rav additional questions, but I felt comfortable leaving it up to the jury to decide my father-in-law's fate. Rav hit the ball out of the park, and I was more than pleased by his performance. His testimony was better than I could have hoped for.

I called my next set of witnesses: several refuseniks. The first witness was a chain smoker with brown bushy hair and a wrinkled face. When he raised his right hand, you could see permanent stains on his index and third fingers left by decades of smoking cigarettes. He had the raspy voice of a smoker and coughed whenever he spoke.

"Please state your name and address for the court reporter."

"I am Alex Dragunsky."

"Please tell the court what your life was like in Russia before you came to the United States."

"Russians are anti-Semitic. I started to learn about my Jewish heritage in secret, attending classes in people's homes. The more I learned, the more I wanted to practice my religion, free from government interference. Once I applied for an emigration visa, my job was threatened."

"When I applied a second time, I lost my job and then I was arrested. They threatened my wife and demanded she leave me. My uncle was a high-ranking military war hero. He came to visit me in jail and pleaded with me to remain a loyal Soviet and to recant my statements about wanting to practice my faith. He instructed me to forget this Jewish nonsense and stop trying to obtain an exit visa. I told him I wanted my freedom and he left."

"In jail, I was left naked and regularly beaten. Finally, after several months I was told I could leave, but I was ordered to divorce my wife. My jailers told me I would never be allowed to have contact with my two children. I took my visa and prayed I would be able to get my wife and children visas to join me in the United States in the future."

Dragunsky took a deep breath. He looked glum. Recounting the past was hard for him. "I have not seen my wife and children since I left the Soviet Union. I have attempted to visit Russia so I could visit with them, but my entry into the Soviet Union was denied. Today, I operate a small engineering company in Maryland that employs ten workers."

I probed him further. "How did you come to the United States?"

"A flight from Prague. Because I wanted to get my children out of the Soviet Union, I was told if I went to the United States rather than Israel, I would have better chances of winning their freedom. I met with people from the Genesis Trust, and they arranged for me to get a visa, a green card and transportation to the United States."

"Do you know Rabbi Lefkovitz?"

"Yes, we met here in the states. The rabbi never told me he was responsible for my visa. Instead, he asked me to advise him so more Soviet Jews would be able to leave."

"What did you tell him?"

"I told him U.S. government pressure on the Soviet regime was essential if we wanted to free more Soviet

Jews. He invited me to sit on his board of directors of his organization so I could assist him. If not for Rabbi Lefkovitz, I would be without hope of ever seeing my family again. Without this good rabbi's actions many of the other Soviet Jews would be without hope today."

Simon wisely chose not to cross examine this witness. The judge adjourned the court for the rest of the day. Within an hour the newspaper headlines proclaimed, 'Rabbi is a hero — saved Jewish lives'.

Someone from the A.G.'s office told me of phone call that Simon received. "Wrap this trial up quickly! The media coverage is not favorable. It is causing problems with our friends in Moscow!"

That night, back at my place I overheard a disturbance in the bathroom. I asked Rav if I could be of help and he said it was nothing but indigestion. I went into the bathroom after he finished and found droplets of blood on the toilet and floor. I told Shira what I saw and heard.

Together we faced him. Shira emphatically told her father, "We are going to take you to the hospital now! Get dressed." I went to reach for his coat from the closet and he stopped me.

He was composed as he shook his head and waved no with his right hand. "Children, remember when I told you the story of Rabbi Shim'on? I told you then my time has come. God has allowed me these precious months to restore my good name before he requires my service in His holy court." He restrained a cough and continued.

"Michael, you and Shira are the only ones who know I am dying."

"In the coming week, I will call my children and grandchildren together to bless each one. Your son, Ben, will become a great legal mind. Yehuda's son, Isaac, will be a world-renowned teacher of the Zohar and respected sage. It is Yehuda who will be my heir apparent at the yeshiva after I depart this world. I want my money in the box I entrusted to Shira to be used to further Isaac's education. I will arrange with the world-renowned scholars Rav Feinstein and Rav Soloveitchik to provide Isaac the best possible learning."

Shira sobbed as I held her hand tightly. "Aba let me take you to the hospital. They may be able to treat you, maybe cure you."

He smiled. "My dearest one, I will be with your mother, God be willing in the near-future. I have seen the doctors and they are surprised I have lasted this long."

That night, while all the health drama played out in our condo, Simon enjoyed the pleasures Rachel had promised him. Rachel called the office and left a brief message with my after-hours answering service. "This message is for Michael. Simon enjoyed himself tonight."

# The trial was ending

The trial resumed the next day. I was prepared to call my four remaining refusenik witnesses to testify. Simon looked a little tired when he approached the bench and said, "For the sake of time, the government will concede that the refuseniks will testify their lives were miserable and brutal in Russia, and if not for the rabbi, the refuseniks would have suffered."

I agreed to the stipulation and the jury was so instructed. I had to decide if I wanted to call any other witnesses. I conferred with Ariel and Rav and we decided to end the trial on a high note.

The testimony phase of the trial had concluded, and it was time for Simon and me to personally address the jury with our final arguments. The judge asked if the parties were ready to present their closing arguments. We said yes. The judge then instructed Simon to proceed with his remarks to the jury. As the prosecutor, Simon was required to give his closing arguments first.

Simon walked up to the jury with a smile exuding confidence. He was smartly dressed and looked like a Gentlemen Quarterly model. He eyed each of the jurors before he spoke.

"Ladies and Gentlemen of the jury. The

government has presented numerous compelling witnesses who testified against Rabbi Lefkovitz. Congressman Boyle met with the rabbi and traded payments for favors. The first set of favors or bribes allegedly benefited individuals in the Soviet Union. The second set of bribes related to the business of selling green cards and visas to illegal immigrants financially benefiting the rabbi. Who, but Rabbi Lefkovitz, had access to the funds to pay Boyle and order his staff to carry out his demands?" Simon paused and pointed to the defendant as he made his point to the members of the jury.

Amid Simon's closing argument, I suddenly realized who was the mastermind behind the illegal scheme. I whispered to Ariel, my co-counsel. "I will return soon. Cover for me." I briskly walked out of the courtroom over to a payphone and telephoned Special Agent Johns.

My departure from the courtroom caught the eye of Simon and the jury. It temporarily caught Simon off guard and caused him to momentarily lose his concentration. When I returned to the courtroom, Simon shot me a dirty glance.

Schwartz continued saying to the jury, "You remember, don't you, we heard from the refugees who benefited from the green cards and visas? Remember the illegal aliens told us they mailed the cashier's checks to the yeshiva and talked to employees at the yeshiva. Who was the head of the yeshiva?" He paused and pointed toward our table with his index finger, and said, "Rabbi Lefkovitz."

Simon turned back to the jury. "We heard from FBI Special Agent Johns and from the FBI handwriting expert. Remember what they told us. They told us the checks paid to Boyle were signed by the rabbi or he allowed the use of his signature stamp to sign them.

Rabbi Lefkovitz' s yeshiva received twelve thousand dollars per month from illegal immigrants. The yeshiva paid four thousand dollars a month to Boyle as bribes. Who but Lefkovitz had the authority to perpetrate this fraud?"

Schwartz walked over to the prosecution table and took a sip of water before continuing. "The yeshiva also paid three thousand dollars to Boyle for campaign contributions each month for thirty-six months. The campaign payments were also bribes because Boyle was being paid to exert his political influence in the issuance of visas. The rabbi used charitable monies to pay the bribes. We all know who ran and oversaw the yeshiva's operations, don't we?" Again, he pointed in the direction of Rav.

"If it was legal and ethical, why did the rabbi transfer the monies to overseas entities? To hide what he was doing from the IRS and the U.S. government?

Simon maintained a sincere facial appearance to win over the jury as he said, "I need you, the jury, to send a message to this rabbi and to all others like him who wish to abuse the laws of our great country. Clergy must not be allowed to misuse charitable contributions for their own personal gain. Finally, clergy must not be allowed to bribe public officials! No one is above the law."

He concluded with, "By finding Rabbi Lefkovitz guilty you are standing up for our laws and our country. Bad actions deserve to be punished. Find Rabbi Moshe Lefkovitz guilty of all the charges. Let him reflect on his violations of the public's trust in prison. Thank you for patiently sitting through this long trial." Simon nodded toward the jury and returned to his table.

Judge Weinberg looked at the clerk, took a sip of water and signaled for me to proceed with my closing argument, without the court taking a morning break.

I walked up to the jury box with a grin on my face; I shook my head as I slowly approached the jurors. I pointed to Simon and said, "Mr. Schwartz, I don't think sending an innocent man to prison is delivering the message we want to convey here in America. Do you? We have here a real-life American hero. A man who has saved lives. How many lives have you saved, Mr. Schwartz?" I let my words sink in with the jury.

The judge interrupted me as he admonished me to direct my arguments to the jury and not Simon. The judge gave me permission to continue with my closing remarks. Fortunately, I had scored points with the jury and that's what counted.

"Yes, we heard from numerous individuals and experts. We heard from Boyle who physically met with the rabbi on one occasion along with other religious leaders. And yes, other religious leaders made donations to Boyle to save Soviet Jewish lives but none of them are on trial here today. Boyle did not tell anyone about campaign financing laws because he needed the monies to get re-elected." Another pause was called for, so I walked around a bit, looking toward the heavens before resuming.

"Boyle allowed himself to be bribed by someone, but it wasn't the good rabbi. Who bribed Boyle? Neither Boyle nor the prosecution were able to identify the young person who was the mastermind behind the illegal visa scheme. This was presumably the same young person who cashed the checks at the currency exchange."

I turned to Simon momentarily. "Mr. Schwartz, it was your witnesses who told us there were three other people at the yeshiva who had the opportunity and the financial authority to have concocted and operated this criminal scheme and bribe Boyle. The rabbi was not one of them. We heard Mayer, the controller at the yeshiva, who testified Rabbi Lefkovitz had no knowledge of the yeshiva's accounting system or how to use the computer. He said that the rabbi didn't even know where the blank checks were kept."

"In fact, the immigrants who paid for green cards testified that they spoke to a younger man. The currency exchange employees who transacted the cashing of checks testified they dealt with a younger man. If you look at Rabbi Lefkovitz and his gray beard, no one could confuse him with being or sounding youthful. Sorry, Rabbi." The jury smiled in agreement.

"The FBI financial experts traced the payments to Boyle to the yeshiva. Yet they failed to find one witness who could identify Rabbi Lefkovitz as the person who committed this illegal act. The gross income test performed by the FBI positively indicated that Rabbi Lefkovitz led a modest lifestyle and didn't spend monies beyond his modest salary. Finally, we heard from Russian refuseniks whose lives were saved by the rabbi and the good people who supported his endeavors. They all thanked Rabbi Lefkovitz for allowing them to be free. Mr. Schwartz, we should have more good men and women like Rabbi Lefkovitz. Then the world would be a better place."

I moved closer to the jury to make my next point. "The rabbi freely admitted making campaign payments to Congressman Boyle, but he didn't know they were in violation of any federal campaign laws. Why would Boyle approach charitable entities for monies if it were illegal? I guess that is a question for Boyle to answer."

"You may ask why the rabbi formed different entities like Exodus and Genesis to conduct business overseas. The reason is simple. The yeshiva couldn't legally participate in payments to foreign government officials. The trust was established to funnel payments in exchange for Soviet exit visas. Genesis was needed to set up the Swiss bank account transfers of money.

Was it legal? I say yes! These actions, as witnesses testified, saved lives." I extended my arms straight out to the sides and asked, "Isn't the saving of a life the greatest act that we can do?"

I concluded my remarks. "Ladies and gentlemen of the jury, thank you for your patience during this long trial. Today is the day you have the power to free this innocent man and permit him to return to his family. I pray you will find him not guilty on all charges. By declaring Rabbi Lefkovitz not guilty you will permit him to continue his mission to free those Jews and other victims of religious persecution in the Soviet Union." I took a deep breath, nodded my head and smiled at the jury before I returned to my seat.

Judge Weinberg gave the jury their instructions. He explained the rule of law on each count. He carefully instructed the jury to consider all the facts presented in the case and not to assume facts not presented at trial. The judge defined legal terms relating to the charges and read the patented jury instructions. The judge continued to educate the jury on the standard of proof the jurors should apply to this case: "Beyond a reasonable doubt." With that, the jury left the courtroom and began deliberations.

After an hour of waiting around the courthouse, Rav and I left, and took a cab to my office, some fifteen minutes away. Shira and her sisters remained in the courtroom praying as they did every day of the trial for their father. Shira told me she and her sister would stay for an additional hour just in case the jury quickly returned with a verdict.

I informed the clerk of the court I would be in my office and asked the clerk to call me if or when the jury indicated they had decided Rav's fate.

When I arrived at my office, I found four sets of movies and photographs. I had Pat type labels on three of the packages and had them delivered by messenger to reporters I trusted working at three separate news agencies. The name of the sender and the return address was excluded from the envelopes. I hoped that these pictures would bring about morning fireworks in the form of headlines.

Rav looked up from his reading text and asked, "How long does it normally take for the jury to come to a decision on a case?"

"It's the worst part of my job. Sometimes they can sit in deliberation for hours and sometimes weeks. It depends on the facts, amount of evidence and the mood of the jurors."

"Is it good for us if it's longer or shorter?"

"It makes no difference." Our conversation was interrupted by a phone call from F.B.I. Special Agent Johns.

Johns started the conversation. "He quit and is no longer working at the yeshiva. He has moved and his apartment is vacant. Two weeks ago, he traded in his car for a new one and paid the difference in cash. We are presenting the facts as we know to the U.S. attorneys' office. I expect they will be presenting it to a grand jury. Thank you for the assistance. Your hunch appears to be right on the mark." After replacing the telephone handle on the receiver, I shared the conversation with Rav. He nodded his head as if to say he wasn't surprised.

At six o'clock, the clerk called to inform me the jury had retired for the night. Assuming that the jury rendered a decision the next day, the court would resume Thursday at the earliest because the judge announced he was not holding court on Wednesday."

Rav and I returned to the condo. Shira and her sisters were there waiting for us. Rav told his daughters that he wanted to host a mandatory family meeting tomorrow night here at the condo. He expected everyone to attend including the youngest of grandchildren.

Wednesday night, the entire Lefkovitz family was in attendance. The Rav kept the agenda he had close to the vest and refused to tell anyone. Shira and I kept his secret.

We had reserved the large room on the ground floor of our condo building to host the Rav's event. From the frosting windows, we could see signs of a cold weather front approaching and heard the gusts of wind.

The delivery man arrived and placed the food on the six-foot long table draped with colorful tablecloths. Shira's sisters set the tables and opened the food containers. When Shira saw the hot sliced pastrami, her mouth began to water. She pictured a toasted onion

Kaiser roll with pastrami, spicy mustard and a fresh pickle slice entering her mouth. When Shira told her sisters, she craved pastrami since becoming pregnant, they all laughed. It seems all her sisters had the same pregnancy craving.

The entire family wondered why the party was organized before the jury announced their findings but came because it was their father's wish that they attend. They asked the reason for the party and Rav explained that it was a celebration of his life.

He piqued their interest and left them wondering so he further explained. "Children God has called me to join him in the heavens above." Horrified stares filled the room.

One-by-one, he blessed each child in order of their age and then each grandchild. When Yehuda approached, he whispered a prayer for a speedy recovery.

Rav afterwards pontificated, "While the physical body dies, the soul remains alive for as long as his owner's good deeds are remembered. In time, we will all be together again."

Sadness doesn't begin to describe the mood his words conveyed. He continued, "I will always be there in the heavens watching over you and praying for you." He made us promise to bury him and have Emah exhumed and buried beside him on the Mount of Olives in Jerusalem.

He verbally disclosed his wishes once he left us. "I

had a retirement plan with the yeshiva. When I'm found innocent, I want these savings returned to my estate and used to pay for the burial costs, with the remainder divided equally amongst all my children." The mood was somber. The children wailed, saying they would rather have their Aba than all the money in the world.

He quieted them and said, "Michael and Yehuda, will you jointly act as the executors of my estate." We both agreed. "I have met with my attorney and updated my last will and testament to memorialize my wishes."

The mood went from tears to laughter as Aba smiled and shared his fondest memories of each of his children. After reciting numerous stories, he looked at Shira. "And you! You refused to talk until you were almost three years old. We took you to countless doctors and specialists. Then one day you started talking in whole sentences. Since then, no one has stopped you from talking." Everyone in the room burst out in laughter, including Shira.

The young grandchildren all stood in line to be the to hop onto the Rav's knee and vie for his attention. The newest family member was Ava's daughter Yael, now three months. He rocked her to sleep in his arms and kissed her soft, wrinkled forehead.

"My children, I am fortunate to have been blessed with heavenly incredible children and grandchildren. I appreciate the time God has permitted me and have gotten to know each of you. Please, never forget to love one another and care for each other all your days on earth. I expect you to carry on the tradition of maintaining a good ethical God-fearing family." With that the evening concluded.

# The verdict

The morning headlines painted a portrait of a U.S. assistant attorney who indulged in kinky and wild sex parties. There were photographs of Schwartz standing naked on a bed over two women handcuffed to the bed frame and others where he was whipping women's backsides with a horse-riding crop. This photograph drew the greatest outrage among feminist groups. The private parts of the women in the photos were obscured, but the reader got the intended message. After seeing the headlines, Simon's former lovers and ex-wife came forward to tell their stories of being physically abused.

The trial court resumed later that morning. Judge Weinberg looked at the foreman and asked, "Has the jury reached a verdict on the multiple criminal counts?" The jury foreman acknowledged that the jury had come to a decision on all counts except one. The foreman stood and handed the jury's decisions to the clerk of the court who in turn gave the envelope to the judge.

"Foreman of the jury, has the jury exhausted all efforts to come to a verdict on the final count?"

"Yes, Your Honor."

The judge looked to the prosecution's table and noticed Simon was missing. The two other U.S.

assistant attorneys were seated at the table in his place. The judge lowered his glasses and remarked, "I guess Mr. Schwartz is auditioning to become a 'Forty-Second Street' film star." The courtroom was filled with laughter. Even Rav had to grin. The judge cleared his throat twice after laughing at his own sense of humor and recomposed himself.

Soberly the judge looked at the defense table. Judge Weinberg asked, "Will the defendant please rise and face the jury."

Both Ariel and I joined Rabbi Lefkovitz as he stood, facing the jury. The foreman was instructed to read the jury's verdict on each count.

The elderly foreman stood tall in his neat gray suit. In a loud voice he began, "Count one: Money Laundering. The jury finds the defendant not guilty.

"Count two: Bribery of a Public Official. The jury finds the defendant not guilty.

"Count three: The Illegal Sale of Government Property. The jury finds the defendant not guilty." At this point I was ready to jump out of my shoes and scream with joy. Out of the corner of my eye, I saw Shira, whose eyes were closed while she and her three sisters continued praying.

"Count four: The Charge of Violating Campaign Financing Laws. The jury has been hopelessly deadlocked."

Judge Weinberg addressed the jury. "I want to thank you, the men and women of the jury, for your hard work and patience. This has been a long trial and your service is appreciated. You are now dismissed."

With an expression of remorse, Judge Weinberg looked directly at the rabbi and said, "Rabbi Lefkovitz, I know this ordeal has been tragic and a difficult time for you and your family. I wish I had the words to comfort you other than by proclaiming you are a free man. I know no one will be able to repair the damage and pain you have endured."

Before the judge adjourned the court, I spoke up. "Your Honor, one more issue."

"Yes, what is that?"

"Rabbi Lefkowitz's bank accounts were seized by court order before the trial commenced. Will the court now issue an order commanding the government to return all the rabbi's funds forthwith?"

"Mr. Goldman write up the order. Give it to my clerk and I will sign it today." With that, the judge stood and retired from the bench. Court was adjourned.

We walked out of the courthouse. There were no reporters outside waiting for us. It was no longer a story people cared to read about. The findings of the jury were buried in a small paragraph in the back of the next day's morning newspaper. It was a chilly November day toward the end of a historic year. Much happened in 1972, however this case faded from peoples' minds and memories.

The government decided to drop all the charges against Yehuda. The yeshiva Bol Shuva begged Rav to return to his old position as their figurehead. He demanded as a precondition that the yeshiva pay his deferred pension funds to him. In paying Rabbi Lefkovitz his pension funds, the yeshiva's coffers were nearly dried up.

Simon called my friend Sam, hoping Sam would represent him on sexual assault charges after Simon's law license was suspended. Sam declined the engagement. That month Sam joined my firm as a partner.

Rav passed-on to the next world one month later, surrounded by his loving family. On that day it was a bright sunny day with blue skies and the birds were singing. It was a moonless night, unusually dark and devoid of stars. The newspapers eulogized him as a good, learned man and a great leader. Yet, there are those who continued to believe the rumors that he was an embezzler who beat the rap.

According to his wishes, we buried him and Emah in Israel, on the Mount of Olives, a three-thousand-year-old cemetery cited in the Jewish and Christian bibles. On day of the burial, a ray of sunlight appeared, and two doves perched on a tree to watch the burial ceremony.

We followed the procession down the steep steps on the Mount of Olives to their final resting place. Thousands attended, including refuseniks, heads of state and many famous individuals. We gave Ben a plastic shovel so he could participate in the ritual of filling in the grave with earth.

We sat shiva and observed the seven-day mourning period in Jerusalem at the King David Hotel. It was surprising how many people came to pay their respects. People came from all over the world to tell us stories of how Rav had impacted their lives. He was too humble to ever mention to any of us these many deeds of loving kindness while he was living.

One evening after the guests had left, Shira turned to me and asked, "How did you know who committed the embezzlement?"

"First of all, only three people had access to the post office box: Yehuda, David Ben Aaron and Mayer. All three of them handled the yeshiva's deposits and check writing. All three requested and had Rav sign checks."

"On the day I met with your Aba as he was giving me advice before our wedding day, I remembered David had rushed into the office. I thought it was bit odd at the time that he barged into the room only after we were in the midst of a serious conversation. He said it was urgent that Rav sign checks without seeing the supporting back up. Rav mentioned that the checks had been sitting on David's desk all day."

"There was only one person who could write checks to Boyle payable to cash and hide his trail by recording the payments in the general ledger of the yeshiva and that was David. He recorded all the computer transactions, and when people called the yeshiva the office staff directed the callers to David. It was David who agreed to testify against Yehuda."

We stayed in Israel for several additional days after the shiva period and enjoyed visiting historical and biblical sites. On the airplane home from Israel, I looked over at Shira who was engrossed in reading one of her romantic novels. Ben was in the seat beside her sleeping.

Shira had a tear fall down her face as she smiled. "Rav loved all of us. He will always be with us."

In June, our second son was born. He was a healthy child. At his bris, we named him Moshe. Named after Rabbi Moshe Lefkovitz. Ava, the oldest of Shira's sisters, assumed certain family responsibilities after Emah's death. She was the first guest to enter Shira's room to visit our son at the hospital. She immediately attached the red thread around my son's tiny wrist. This time I had no objections.

# Epilogue

Simon Schwartz was punished for his sins. He lived in a depressive hell with no friends for a few years. He lost his license to practice law and was unemployable. Eventually, he dissipated his savings and was subjected to numerous lawsuits from his ex-wife who chased him for back child support and spousal maintenance. He took his own life one December evening. Few attended his funeral.

The struggle to save Soviet Jews continued because of Rabbi Lefkovitz, Senator Henry (Scoop) Jackson from Washington and Representative Charles A. Vanik from Ohio. These elected officials sponsored an amendment to the Trade Act of 1974. The law denied the Soviet Union 'Most favored nation' status. This status prevented countries with restrictive emigration policies and laws from trading goods with the United States without tariffs and restrictions.

Senator Jackson and Vanik introduced the amendment in 1972. It took three years of pressuring Congress and the Senate before the Jackson Vanik amendment was signed into law in 1975 by Gerald Ford. The law successfully forced Russian and the other Eastern bloc nations into ending the physical and